HUE AND CRY

HUE AND CRY

HUE AND CRY

THOMAS B. DEWEY

#1 in the Singer Batts series

WILDSIDE PRESS

Hue and Cry was also published as *Room for Murder*.

CHAPTER 1

I don't know how many times the bell rang before I woke up. I was dead asleep that night and the night bell doesn't make a lot of racket anyway. The first thing I knew I had the sheet wound around my neck, the telephone in one hand, and I was saying, "Hello, hello," over and over as fast as I could. Then I caught on that it was the night bell, not the telephone, and I hung up and found my slippers, pulled on my pants and a sweat shirt, and went into the sitting room.

The light was on in there and Singer was still up. He was sitting at his little desk over against the wall between the two big windows, working away on something I didn't know about and probably wouldn't have understood anyway.

I looked at my watch. (I sleep with it on, ever since one time when the telephone rang at three o'clock in the morning and somebody asked me for the time. I told him to go to hell, and the next morning I found out it was the only really permanent guest the hotel had and he moved out that day and never came back.) It was two-forty-five. I had been in bed for four hours. I couldn't remember when Singer had been in bed. I think this was the twenty-third straight hour without sleep. It might have been more or less.

"It's two-forty-five," I said. "Why don't you go to bed?"

No answer.

"Singer," I said, "I don't care if you ruin your health, but I got a job to think of. If you pass out what happens to me?"

He looked around then, very serious. "But I've told you many times, Joe, that if anything happens to me the hotel will go to you. You'll own it."

I stared at him.

"I thought you went to bed a long time ago," he said. "I did."

"I see."

Never wait for Singer Batts to ask a personal question. He doesn't operate that way. You live your life, he'll live his. It's only when there's something he thinks he's got a right to know that he'll ask questions. Then he'll ask plenty. Questions to drive you crazy.

"I did go to bed a long time ago," I said.

"Have I kept you awake?"

"Hell no, friend. The bell rang."

"The bell?"

"As manager of this hotel," I said, "in which you take such a tremendous interest that you don't even know I got a bell in my room that the night clerk can ring if he wants me."

A look of horror came over Singer's face. "Your grammar gets worse all the time, Joe. You didn't even *try* to finish that sentence."

The bell rang again in my room, twice.

"Grammar," I said. "About grammar I don't know nothing." (I did that on purpose. I know better, really.) "Anyway, that sentence was getting too long."

"So you have a bell," Singer said.

"Sure. Hear it?"

"Yes. There must be a pin in it. Who's on the other end?"

"Our night clerk. Fellow name of Jack Pritchard. Been working here for twenty years. Your old man hired him. Remember?"

"He must be the man who used to peel apples for me when I was a child," Singer said. "Nice old man... You'd better see what he wants, I guess. That must be hard on the battery—or whatever it is that makes a bell ring."

"Sure," I said. "I'll go right away. Probably wants to know what happened to that paper clip that was on the desk when he came to work."

"Never criticize people for being conscientious, Joe."

"You better go to bed," I said, and went on into the lobby.

Pritchard was sitting on the bell all right, but the reason for it was bigger than a paper clip. The reason was big Pete Haley, the town marshal, and he was having quite a time. He was standing in the middle of the lobby hanging onto two kids by their collars. He had one at the end of each arm. They kept trying to get away. They'd start to turn around and swing on Pete and he'd give them a little twist and they'd jerk back into position, all the time cussing at him and carrying on. He had such a tight grip on them by now that their faces were bright red.

All the time, Pete kept saying over and over: "Now, boys, calm down, stiddy there, calm down, take back a little. Remember your father, remember your mother, take back a little..." And every time he had to give them another twist, he'd say, "Stiddy there, whoa, boys."

It was pretty funny at first and I started to laugh, and then all of a sudden I thought, "What the hell is he doing bringing them in the hotel like this?"

I walked over and stood just out of reach of those kids' arms. I recognized them as a couple of high-school boys from respectable families. I couldn't remember their names.

Pete looked across his big belly and saw me.

"What's the matter?" I said. "The drugstore cowboys get a little too much?"

"They ain't bad kids," Pete said right away.

"Who said they were?" I said. "What are they doing in here?"

"I brought 'em in," Pete said. "Had to do somethin'—way they was carryin' on out on the street."

"You've got a jail right down the street," I said. "Hasn't been used for fifteen years. Why not take them down there?"

"Now, Joe," Pete said, "you know it would hurt these kids' folks if they was to turn up in jail. No need for it—no need to hang a record on 'em. I thought, maybe—"

Pete had done this before. The big softy couldn't stand it to enforce the law. Luckily in Preston it didn't make much difference.

"You thought maybe you'd like to put 'em up here and let 'em sleep it off?"

"Well—yeah—that is, 'course I'll pay."

I started to say, "You're damned right you'll—" then I looked at Pete's big, round, baby face. "Okay, the hell with it," I said.

One of the kids swung on Pete, twisted and got away. He headed out, tripped over Pete's foot, and stumbled into the desk. I caught him and straightened him up. Then he swung on me and hung a beauty right on the side of my face. I grabbed his arms—little spindly arms, felt like they'd splinter if I put any pressure on—and held him off. He jerked and twisted and cussed me out and glared at me, and blew his breath in my face. Then he did something I don't like. He spit at me.

"All right, Junior," I said and lifted him off the floor. "You quiet down, or Uncle Joe will let you have it right in the teeth."

I shook him a little and he cooled off some. But he still glared at me and ran off at the mouth, talking thickly and not making any sense. Then he started twisting again and kicking at me. He had the very devil in him.

"Cut it out," I said, and I slapped him hard across the face.

"Now, take it easy, Joe," Pete said. "No need to hurt him."

"I'll kill him," I said, "if he doesn't stand still."

Jack Pritchard, a little thin, dried-up old man with snow-white hair and wearing a bow tie and a celluloid collar, stood behind the desk and shook his head slowly. He looked at Pete with his kid and me with mine and then he put his hands in his pockets and looked at the ceiling.

"Any vacancies?" I asked him—as if I didn't know.

Jack Pritchard just sneered.

"Well?" I said.

"Ten vacancies," he said. "Most of 'em are way upstairs on the third, fourth, and fifth floors, which is as high as this here hotel goes. But there's one on the second floor, right up at the head of the stairs. Number 7."

I looked at Pete.

"How you going to make them sleep it off?" I said. "You going to tie them to the bed?"

"Well, I figured we'd sober 'em up first—give 'em a cold bath—"

"Give 'em a bath?" I said. "Who? You going to call up their mothers and get *them* down here?"

"Now, Joe, 'twouldn't be much trouble—"

"I've got guests in this hotel," I said. "I should just drag a couple of village idiots upstairs, turn on the water, throw 'em in and let 'em yell?"

One of the kids started talking sense.

"Listen," he said. "Don't put me in any cold water. Please. I can't stand it. I'm all right now. I'm sober." Pete let go of him. The kid took three steps and fell flat on his face. He just lay there.

The one I was holding gave up the struggle. I gave him a little push and he slid down against the desk and sat on the floor.

"Maybe they'll go to sleep after all," I said.

"Why, sure," said Pete, proudly. "They're good kids."

"Oh, my God!" I said. "I'll take this one upstairs, Pete, and you take care of the one that passed out."

"Sure," said Pete.

"Stand up, Junior," I said to the kid, taking hold of his collar.

He came up all right and walked across the lobby without any squawk. But when we got to the bottom of the stairs he stopped and hung back.

"Where you taking me?" he said.

"Go along, son," Pete said. "You'll be all right. Get a good night's sleep."

"I don't want to stay," he said. "You got no right."

"He's got a right to throw you in jail for thirty days," I said. "Now come on so I can get back to sleep."

"No," he said.

"What are you afraid of?" I said. "You'll be in a nice hotel room, with a traveling salesman on one side and a beautiful schoolteacher on the other—"

"Miss Mason?"

"Yeah."

"Yeah?"

"This could go on forever," I said. "Come on."

He came right along, as quiet as you please, tiptoeing upstairs. I got out my master key and opened the door to Number 7. It was a warm May night and there was a bright moon. It flooded into the room, lighting up the old steel bed and the chair beside it and the dresser over by the wall near the window. I snapped on the light and the moonlight disappeared.

"Take off your clothes," I said, "and give them to me."

"What the hell?" the kid said.

"Never mind," I said. "Just do what I tell you."

He was swaying a little on his feet and his eyes were staring. There was a bright little pin-point of light in the middle of each eye.

He took off his coat and handed it to me. Then his tie and shirt. He looked at me staring at him and squirmed a little.

"What are you staring at?" he said. "Don't a guy get any privacy?"

"You're not just drunk," I said.

"No?" he said. "So what?"

I studied him. After a couple of minutes he looked away.

"I've got you now," I said. "You're Roy Blake, Joshua Blake's kid."

His eyes jerked back to mine. "You wouldn't squeal to my old man, would you?"

"Give me the rest of your clothes and get in bed."

He started to put his hand in his pants pocket.

"Oh, no," I said. "Everything."

Reluctantly he took off his pants and tossed them to me. He sat down on the edge of the bed to take off his shoes and socks. I heard Pete Haley puffing up the stairs. He came pushing through the door just as the Blake kid handed me his shoes and socks and drew his feet up under him on the bed. Pete was carrying the other kid like a baby in his arms. He dumped him on the bed beside the Blake kid. Roy Blake looked at him without expression.

"Who is he?" I asked Pete.

"He's Harley Granger's kid, Sam."

Harley Granger owned the hardware store and some real estate. He was well off.

"Well," I said to Pete, "take off young Master Granger's clothes and come down to the lobby. Bring the clothes with you and my master key—after you've locked the door."

"Bring the clothes?" Pete said stupidly. He was still breathing hard from the stair-climbing.

"Yeah," I said. "All of them."

Roy Blake looked at me, pleading. I figured it wouldn't do him any harm to worry a little, so I just gave him a stony stare. As I started out the door, he called, "Hey!"

I stopped without turning around.

"Hey," he said, "does Miss Mason live down at the end of the hall there, at the front?"

"Yeah. What about it?"

He whistled.

"Shut up," I said. "You go to bed and keep quiet. If there's any racket in here I'll call up your old man and tell him to come and get you. And Pete," I said, thinking of the lovely Miss Mason, "don't forget to lock the door."

"All right, all right, Joe," Pete said. He had already started to take off the Granger kid's clothes.

I went downstairs to the desk with young Blake's clothes wadded up under my arm. I laid them on the desk and said to Jack Pritchard: "There'll be some more of these. Put them on the lost-and-found shelf and we'll give them back to the punks when they wake up."

Pritchard lifted his nose. "In the old days—" he began.

"In the old days," I said, having no respect for age, "it was the same thing. Wasn't it?"

He sniffed. I had never got along with Pritchard, but he stayed on as night clerk because one of the provisions of the will by which Emory Batts left the Preston Hotel to his son, Singer, was that Jack Pritchard should have the job as long as he wanted it. It was easy to see that Pritchard was going to want it for the rest of his life. He was the damnedest old maid I'd ever known and he drove me nuts with his superior airs and righteousness, but he was honest. And he never went to sleep on the job—which is more than I could say for the day clerk. Pete came downstairs with Sam Granger's clothes. "Give 'em to Jack, Pete. We'll take them up to the kids when they wake up."

"What's the idea of that, Joe?" Pete said.

"Just a little insurance," I said. "I don't want them banging around in the hotel, and you don't want them back on the street again."

Pete gave me my master key.

"I appreciate this, Joe," he said. "Mind if I use your telephone? Want to call the kids' folks, tell 'em they're all right. No need to worry 'em."

"What a copper!" I said. "Go ahead. You're off duty at midnight. Don't you ever sleep?"

"Oh, sure. I'm going home soon as I finish these calls."

"Good night," I said.

Pete picked up the phone. And to Jack Pritchard I said: "Don't ring that bell again. If we catch fire, just send the boys in after me."

This was not Jack Pritchard's idea of a joke. He sniffed. As I went off toward the suite I could hear Pete Haley fussing around with his explanations as to why Roy Blake hadn't come home yet. What a copper!

Singer was still at it. I went over to the table and looked at what he was doing. He had an old book that looked like it was about to fall apart and some sheets of paper covered with scrawls.

"What's that?" I said.

Singer laid down his pencil and folded his hands.

"It's a murder case out of the sixteenth century. One of Queen Elizabeth's maids—killed in her bed. Nobody ever solved it."

"Maybe she bit him," I said.

There was a long silence. Then Singer said slowly: "I have been assuming all along that she was killed by a woman—even Elizabeth herself. But why? Maybe you are right, Joe. Maybe it was a man and perhaps she did bite him."

"Oh, God," I said. "Now you'll never get to bed."

I started toward my own room.

"What was the trouble?" Singer asked.

"The trouble?"

"Why did your bell ring?"

I turned around. "You're interested?" I said.

"Of course."

"Okay. A couple of young blades about town were raising hell with the public peace. Jovial Pete Haley couldn't stand it to throw them into the clink. He brought them over here so we could put them up for the night."

"And did we?"

"Yes, sir," I said, "right between the traveling salesman from Detroit and a beautiful schoolteacher, the lovely Miss Marion Mason."

"You think they'll be safe?"

"The kids—they'll be safe. I don't know about the others."

"Oh?"

"They weren't just drunk. They were hopped up. Marijuana."

Singer blinked.

"Figure that one out," I said. "I'm going to bed." And I did.

CHAPTER 2

I slept later than usual that morning and didn't get into the sitting room until nine o'clock. Singer was still up, his thin shoulders hunched over the table, his head resting on his hands, looking like a human question mark, trying to figure out a murder that happened three hundred years ago.

"Had any breakfast?" I said.

He didn't even answer and I didn't press the point. I don't like to talk before breakfast anyway.

I went out to the kitchen and got something to eat and told Dora, the cook, to take something in to Singer.

"And make him eat it," I said, "if you have to feed him with a spoon."

Dora sighed and clumped off to find a tray.

"I declare," she said, "that Singer Batts wouldn't live three days if you wasn't around to look after him."

"Skip it," I said. "He got along all right before I turned up."

"Not very good, he didn't. He used to go two days at a time without eating a thing. Never went to bed."

"He still don't go to bed. But some people don't need much sleep."

"Look how skinny he is," Dora said. "He ought to eat a lot—fatten up."

"His brain's fat enough to make up for it."

"Nobody's that smart," she said, "that they don't have to eat."

"Okay."

I finished the last of my toast and coffee and lit a cigarette. It was nine-twenty, and I had some bookkeeping to do before I went to the bank, which would close today, Saturday, at noon. But I went into the lobby first to check up on the early morning events.

The only guy in the lobby was Harry Baird, the day clerk, and he was asleep. His face was red as a beet, which meant he was sleeping one off. Once-a-week Baird we called him. It never failed. Every Friday night. He never got in any trouble, just sat somewhere and got polluted. I hated to wake the old guy up, but—business is business. I stepped up to the desk and slammed my hand down hard. Old Harry came up out of his chair, clawing at the desk.

"Morning, Harry," I said.

"Goldang it!" he said. "Joe, I wish you'd quit that bangin' on the desk. I wake up easy. Just a little tap or two—"

"I've tried those little taps or two," I said. "Anything happen this morning?"

"Nope. Quiet as a grave. Nobody in—nobody out—"

"Yeah, yeah," I said. "I know."

"Mebbe something tomorrow," Harry said.

"I've heard that before, too. Try to stay awake, Harry. Might be some beautiful movie star would come in—"

"In this one-horse, moth-eaten hick town?" said Harry. "Don't make me laugh."

"Okay."

"Nothin' ever happens here."

"All right, Harry. Take it easy. Watch that blood pressure."

"Goldang it," he muttered. "Every day you wake me up and every day it's for nothin'."

I glanced at the lost-and-found shelf under the desk. "I see the boys got their clothes," I said. "They slept that one off in a hurry."

"What boys?"

I looked at him. "What time did you come on this morning?" I asked.

"Seven o'clock, same as usual."

He shifted his eyes.

"Wasn't there a bundle of clothes on the shelf there?"

"What are you talkin' about?" he said.

"You been on the desk steady, ever since you came in?"

"Certainly."

"You didn't get a call from Number 7, to bring up some clothes?"

"No. I never heard anything about any clothes."

I thought it over for a minute. "Well," I said, "maybe Jack Pritchard took them up."

"Yeah, maybe he did." Harry looked at me as though I were crazy.

That must be it, I thought, as I walked away. But I can't figure out how they woke up so early—unless they just didn't go to sleep. But that Granger kid was out cold. Or was he?

The hell with it, I thought, and went into the sitting room. Singer had eaten something, all right. But he hadn't let it disturb him any. There were crumbs all over his table and the tray was perched on the edge, within an inch of sliding off onto the floor. I took it off the table and set it on the floor beside my desk, which was against the wall opposite Singer's table. I snapped on my green-shaded lamp and got out my ledger. But I found myself staring at the wall.

Those two kids couldn't have been awake at seven o'clock—unless—

"Singer," I said quietly, without turning around.

After a moment he said, "Yes, Joe?"

I thought about it. "Nothing," I said. "Why don't you go to bed?"

"I will, pretty soon. I've been working on your theory."

"My theory of what?"

"Of this Elizabethan murder—the theory that it was a man who did the killing."

"Oh," I said. "Why shouldn't it be a man?"

"I think it was," he said.

"I see."

"Do you, Joe?"

"Sure."

"Why couldn't it have been a woman?"

"You trapped me," I said. "Keep this up and *I'll* go to bed. For a long time."

Singer was laughing softly.

"You're very ingenious, Joe. Why don't you hire a manager for the hotel and come into partnership with me?"

"You make me nervous," I said. "Go to bed."

"Does it really mean so much to you, my going to bed?"

I shrugged. "Only that you make me nervous."

Singer sighed. I could hear him rattling his papers.

His chair scraped back and he stood up, bumping his knee against the under side of the table.

"And don't try to sneak that book off to bed with you," I said.

In a little while I heard the book slap the table. Singer shuffled across the room to the door of his bedroom. I watched him out of the corner of my eye. At his door he stopped.

"Joe."

"Yeah?"

"What happened to your two boys—the ones that woke you up this morning?"

I began leafing through my ledger. "I guess they've gone home by now. Must have left just before Harry came on at seven."

I pretended to find my page and studied it. After a while Singer's door opened. He disappeared and it closed again silently. Again I was staring at the wall.

"The guy's uncanny," I said to myself, and jumped at the sound of my own voice.

* * * *

The discouraging thing about looking over the hotel accounts was not really the fact that we made such a little bit of money. Because Singer, with the three-thousand per annum his old man left him along with the hotel, didn't need the money. The discouraging thing was that a lousy seventy-five or eighty bucks' profit in three months made me look like a poor manager. And I knew I wasn't. Of course, Singer knew it too, when he stopped to think about it, and he didn't care anyway. But that didn't help me in my own eyes. So, as usual after looking over the books, I was depressed. When I get depressed, I get sore. And when I'm sore, I'm likely to be rude. And I was rude this morning when Nancy Wheeler came in to clean up the sitting room, dragging her mop and vacuum, with a dust cloth under her arm, singing to herself and staring pop-eyed at everything through her thick glasses.

Not only does Nancy have a hare-lip, so that you have to ask her to repeat everything at least six times. She is also hard of hearing. She said something to me and I didn't get it.

"What?" I yelled.

She said it again, coming closer, staring at me, and I still didn't get it.

"Never mind," I said. "Just go ahead."

So she started to dust off my desk, pushing papers out of the way and picking up my ash tray suddenly so that I missed it and sprinkled ashes all over the books.

"My God!" I said. "Don't start with me. Can't you see I'm working now?"

She looked a little bewildered, but backed away, and started the vacuum. The racket it made got on my nerves. I went over and touched her arm. She turned the thing off.

"You'd better wait till later," I said. "Mr. Batts is trying to sleep."

"Eh?" she said, one hand behind her ear.

I yelled at her. "Mr. Batts is trying to sleep!"

I finally got her out and headed for the guest rooms. Pull yourself together, I thought. What the hell?

But I had a strange feeling, as if I were just hanging around, stalling, waiting for somebody to lay a sap against the back of my neck.

I shut the ledger and put it away. I took out the bank book and a couple of deposit slips and put on my hat.

In the lobby I ran into Pete Haley, his big, rosy face all smiles. He said: "Well, Joe, we'd better get those boys up and dressed. Time they went home."

I looked at him. "Those boys," I said, "are probably no longer here."

Pete's mouth dropped open. "You mean they went already, Toe?"

"Yeah."

I told him about the clothes being gone when Harry Baird came on duty. Pete looked helplessly at Harry, who was asleep again.

"Maybe Jack Pritchard took the clothes up," Pete said.

"Maybe," I said. "Call him up."

Pete hemmed and hawed.

"I ain't so good on the phone."

"All right," I said. "I'll call him."

I got Jack on the phone. He didn't like being waked up. I let him blow off a little steam. Finally he asked, "Well, what is it?"

"Did you take those boys' clothes up to them this morning?" I said.

"I did not."

I looked at Pete, shaking my head.

"Were they still on the shelf when you went off at seven?"

"Seven! That Harry Baird was late again. I wish you'd do something about—"

"Never mind that," I said. "Were they there when you left?"

"No. They were gone."

"Gone? How could they go? Were you on the desk all the time?"

"According to my usual custom," he said, "I went out to the kitchen at three-fifteen to get a snack. Emory Batts always—"

"Yeah, yeah," I said. "All right. Was that the only time you left?"

"No. I was gone for about five minutes a little after five o'clock."

"When did you notice that the clothes were gone?"

"Not till seven-thirty, when Harry Baird finally came in."

"Not till seven-thirty?"

"That's what I said. You ought to talk to Harry—"

"I don't mean about Harry. How does it happen you didn't notice the clothes were gone before?"

I could practically hear old Jack Pritchard drawing himself up.

"The Hotel has never assumed responsibility for articles not placed in the safe," he said. "I am not a watch dog. I am a clerk."

"Okay," I said. "I'm not bawling you out. I'm just looking for information."

He calmed down a little. "Anything else?" he asked.

"I guess not. The clothes could have disappeared between three-fifteen and three-forty-five, or between five and five-oh-five?"

"That is correct."

"Thank you," I said, and hung up.

I told Pete the story.

"But we locked them in," he said. "How was they going to get out?"

"You got me," I said. "Maybe they just oozed out through the keyhole."

Pete dragged out a red bandanna and began to mop his face. It was getting redder all the time.

"I don't know how they did it," I said, "but they must have got hold of the clothes, sneaked down the fire escape and gone home. Maybe they're home right now."

Pete brightened up.

"Mebbe so," he said. "Yeh. I guess mebbe that's where they are. Sure. Naturally."

"Naturally."

But I didn't believe it.

"I'll just hang around awhile," Pete said, "and mebbe their folks will call up and tell me they got home."

"Sure."

Pete clomped out the main entrance. He would sit down on the steps out front and hang around. I wished him luck. I walked around to the safe, opened it and took out the last week's receipts. Harry Baird went right on snoring. I slammed the safe door shut and he didn't even blink. I went around the desk and slammed it with my hand. That got him. He was just as mad as he had been the first time.

"Prop your eyes open," I said. "I'm going to the bank."

He glared at me. "You'd think somebody was going to jump a bill or something."

"Well?" I said.

"Well who?"

"We had a traveling salesman in Number Five last night. I haven't seen him yet."

"Him. He checked out early," Harry said.

"He did?" I said, laying the stuff down on the desk. "Five-thirty. Bill's right here."

"Five-thirty. Funny time for a salesman to check out. Who was he? You ever see him before?"

"Nope. Came around noon yesterday. Carryin' a new line—cutlery. Nice stuff. He showed me."

"Where was he from?"

Harry consulted the register. "Gives a Detroit address."

"Detroit firm he represents?"

"He don't say."

"What's his name?"

"Stephen W. Pfeffer."

"Five-thirty this morning?"

"Yep."

"Okay. Keep your eyes open anyway. Somebody might come in."

"Yeah."

I picked up the pass book and went out the front door. It was a warm spring day. There was a balmy breeze floating down Front Street and the usual gang sitting on the steps. Pete was there, "hanging around," along with half a dozen of the old boys that used to be farmers and now, having sold out and moved into town, lived their last days sitting on the hotel steps in the summer and, in the winter, beside the stove in the harness shop next door. I had once suggested to the ownership that we would do better to build a porch around the steps and turn the place into a sanitarium.

I leaned against the door and listened to the old boys' conversation. There wasn't much of it and what there was didn't amount to anything. Every time somebody walked by the talk would stop and all the heads would turn and follow whoever it was practically out of sight. Then somebody would spit and start talking again.

I twisted around to squint at the little bronze plaque on the brick wall beside the door, wondering whether it would be worthwhile to ask Nancy to polish it up. The plaque read:

HOTEL PRESTON
Owner—Singer Batts
Manager—Joe Spinder

That last name is mine.

I decided against having it polished. I felt a little guilty about Nancy.

I got a good grip on the bank book and went down the steps. On the way I stopped beside Pete Haley and said: "Harry's awake now, but I don't know for how long. If you hear the phone ring, you better go in and make sure it gets answered."

"Oh—sure, Joe. Sure," Pete said.

I went on to the bank. It was cool and quiet in there.

I went up to Tommy Rowe's window.

He was sitting on his stool in the cage, his elbows propped up, his head in his hands. Another hangover. The guy couldn't leave the stuff alone. I remember thinking that if his old man didn't kill him, liquor would. But I knew his father wouldn't kill him. He was too proud. Send him away maybe. He'd bought Tommy out of trouble time and again. Mr. Rowe was too good a businessman to let an investment like that go to waste.

I pushed the book and the dough through the window and said, "Hi, Tommy."

He raised his head slowly and blinked his red eyes at me. He reached for the pass book and counted the spinach. He stamped the deposit slip and dropped the money into a drawer.

"Hello, Joe."

"You look terrible," I said.

"I feel terrible." He handed the book back to me.

"Thanks," I said.

"Joe."

"Yeah?"

He handed me a long white envelope. His hand was shaking so that he almost dropped it.

"Will you put this in Marian's box for me?" he said. "I want her to get it this morning."

"Sure."

I put the envelope in my coat pocket.

"And Joe—" he said, "don't mention it to the old man."

"Okay."

I walked away.

"What the hell," I thought. "You drive a Buick phaeton and run around with the most beautiful babe in town and you can't even let your old man know you wrote her a letter. What a lousy life!"

Mr. Rowe, Tommy's father, a big white-haired guy with a face like old leather and great big hands, looked up and grinned as I went by.

"Morning, Joe," he said. "That old shack of yours still running?"

"That old shack," I said, "will run as long as your bank stays solvent," and grinned back at him.

"You worried about my bank, Joe?"

"No," I said. "Are you?"

He laughed.

Mr. Rowe was all right. I liked being on good terms with him. He was one of the best guys in town to be on good terms with. He had it pretty tough. His kid was a wastrel and his wife had bad heart trouble. Folks said he spent all his spare time taking care of her—like a nurse. But he was always cheerful and he'd kept that bank going great when everybody else's bank was flopping all over the place.

"Seriously," Mr. Rowe said, "how's business?"

"Seriously, it's lousy."

"You ought to work up a few more permanent guests."

"No money in it," I said. "Anyway—who wants to live in an old hotel for six bucks a week when he can rent a whole house for twenty-five a month?"

"Well," he said, "you and Singer get along all right."

"Singer and I—we've got an especially nice set-up. You couldn't get that for six bucks a week."

"Singer's a nice boy," Mr. Rowe said.

"Sure," I said. "But no head for business."

Mr. Rowe sighed.

"Maybe that's all to the good," he said. "Sometimes I wish I had a head for something besides business."

I couldn't think of anything to say to that so I let it pass. And just as I was getting ready to say good-bye to him the door of the bank flew open and in came Harley Granger. He didn't look happy. He was out of breath and his thin lips were twitching. He didn't notice me at first but tore right up to Mr. Rowe's desk.

"Jonathan," he said, "something's got to be done about that damned Pete Haley. Got the sense of a crawfish."

"What's the matter now?" said Mr. Rowe.

I began to get a tight feeling in my stomach.

"Last night," Granger said, "my boy was out with Josh Blake's kid, Roy, and—well, boys will be boys, you know—I guess they'd had a little too much and got to carryin' on. So somebody called Pete and he picked them up."

Mr. Rowe was grinning. "Throw them in jail?" he said.

"Jail nothing," Harley Granger said. "He put 'em up in the hotel."

All of a sudden Mr. Rowe got very serious. He looked at me. Harley Granger saw me then, too.

"What do you know about this, Joe?" he said.

"No more than you do," I said, which was almost true.

Mr. Rowe was staring at me. "Did Pete bring the boys into the hotel?" he said.

"That's right."

"What time?"

"Why—around two-forty-five."

"But why?" said Harley Granger. "Why the hotel?"

"What's wrong with the hotel?" I said.

"The boys have got homes," Granger said.

"Pete was just trying to make it easy for you," I said. "The kids were plastered, raising hell. He didn't want to worry you by bringing them home in that shape. He also didn't want to put them in jail. He paid for the hotel rooms out of his own pocket."

I don't know why I stuck up for Pete that way, but I had never liked Harley Granger and I didn't like his attitude about a poor dumb cop who was only trying to help him out.

"I'll pay my own bills," Granger said.

"Pay Pete," I said. "You don't vote him enough pay to keep him alive anyway."

"He gets more than he's worth."

"Well, what's the rest of it, Harley?" Mr. Rowe said. "There must be something else."

"There is," Granger said. "What I want to know is, where is the kid now?" He stuck out his chin and stared at me.

"He's probably home in bed," I said.

"No, he's not. He never came home. He's not home now, and I don't think he's in town, even."

"What makes you think that?" Mr. Rowe said.

"I got this note, just a few minutes ago. It was in the mail box along with the rest of the mail. Only it hadn't been mailed. It was just dropped in there."

"Let's see it," Mr. Rowe said.

Granger handed him the note. Mr. Rowe read it and passed it to me. It was written in pencil on a piece of hotel stationery and it said:

> I'm going away. Don't try to find me. I'll be all right. I can't stay in this town any longer. Say good-bye to Mom.
>
> Sam

I gave the note back to Granger.

"What do you think of it, Joe?" said Mr. Rowe.

"I don't understand it," I said.

I told them about taking the kids' clothes and locking the door.

"Somebody must have helped them," Mr. Rowe said.

"Yeah, but who?"

"I never did trust that Jack Pritchard," Granger said.

"Pritchard's all right," I said. "He might have given the kids their clothes, but he'd have told me about it—and with pleasure."

"Where's Pete now?" said Mr. Rowe.

"Last I saw of him he was over at the hotel," I said.

"We'd better go over and see him," Mr. Rowe said. "Maybe we'll find some clue as to where the kid went." He got his hat from the rack behind his desk and we went out.

"You think the Blake boy went with him?" Granger said.

Mr. Rowe shrugged. "Maybe. Heard anything from Tosh Blake?"

"No."

Nobody said anything then until we got into the lobby, and by that time nothing that anybody said made much sense.

At first glance, it looked like half the town had swarmed into the lobby. The second look showed me that there were only the half-dozen old duffers from out front, Pete Haley, Harry Baird—awake for once—and Nancy Wheeler. Nancy was carrying on something terrible, throwing her apron over her head and pulling it down again and all the time hollering in that muffled, throaty voice.

I went up to Harry Baird. He was sitting beside Nancy on a sofa, trying to get her calmed down. The o' gaffers were hanging around, chewing and staring. Mr. Rowe and Granger followed me.

"What's up?" I asked Harry Baird.

"Goldang it," he said, "I can't git nothin' out of her. She's been carryin' on like that for five minutes."

"Nancy," I said loudly, "what's the matter?"

She just made more noise and less sense. I shook her a little and she quieted down some. She stared at me with those pop eyes and shivered all over like a scared dog.

"What happened?" I said. "Say it slow."

Her lips moved a lot, but for a long time no sound came out. Then finally she began to make the words.

"That—schoolteacher—" she said.

"Marian Mason?" I said.

She nodded.

"What about her?"

Nancy's lips worked again. "She's—dead."

"Dead?"

"She's dead. Been kilt."

"How do you know she's dead?" I said.

"She's layin' there with a knife in her. There's blood on her!"

Then she went off the deep end again. I looked at Pete Haley. Pete wasn't doing so well. His hat was off and he was mopping his forehead with that bandanna. Everybody else was looking at him, too. He cleared his throat and put his hat on, but he couldn't think of anything to say. I stood up.

"You keep the people out of here, Pete," I said. "Don't let anybody go upstairs and if anybody comes down, don't let them leave. Harry, you take care of Nancy."

Mr. Rowe touched my shoulder.

"I'm acquainted with Weaver, the county attorney," he said. "Suppose I call him?"

"Sure," I said.

"What about my boy?" Harley Granger said.

I turned around and looked at him.

"Yeah," I said. "What *about* your boy?"

Harley Granger looked like he was about to strangle.

"Where are you goin'?" Pete Haley called.

Without stopping, I said, "I'm going to do a little investigating."

I made for the stairs and the second floor. My watch said eleven-forty-five.

CHAPTER 3

Miss Mason's room was to the right at the top of the steps. Number 9. A front room, with south and east windows. I admit that my heart was beating faster than usual. Miss Mason was the town sensation. She had come in the fall, a new teacher in the high school. She was the most beautiful dame to hit Preston in many years, so they told me.

I took out my handkerchief and placed it gently over the knob, twisted it carefully, pushed the door open and walked into the room.

The sight of the undraped female form is a thing men will look for from the time they know what it is until they are in the grave. And I am no exception. But believe me, brother, murder makes a difference. A naked woman is one thing. A naked corpse is something else. It is not anything you want to hang around and stare at.

Miss Mason was not lovely anymore. She was too dead. She lay on her back, her head on a pillow, her auburn hair spread out over it in a tangle. Her arms lay close to her sides and were slightly bent at the elbows. One leg was crossed over the other at her ankles and she was twisted to one side from the hips down. Just under her left breast, the handle sticking straight up, was the knife. It was an ordinary butcher knife, the kind you'll find in any kitchen, a dark brown handle with brass rivets holding it together. There was a thin dark line of blood running from the edges of the wound the knife had made down her side and a little blob of it on the bedspread. It wasn't much.

Her face was gray. Her lips were thin and tight across her teeth. Her eyes were closed.

It all seemed out of joint. The sun streamed in the window. There was a spring smell in the air. You could hear traffic on the street below and the kids playing and yelling at each other.

I found myself looking at Miss Mason's face, saying, "I'm sorry, kid."

Then I jerked my eyes away and looked around the room. The east window was open, the shade up. It gave on a fire escape, an old iron staircase that went straight along the east side of the building to catch each room on that level and then dropped away sharply to the alley in the back. Across the way rose the wall of Mr. Rowe's bank. A dirt area way ran between the bank and the hotel from the street to the alley behind the buildings. I went over to the window and looked at the sill. There was a light film of dust on it and some smudges. I got down close and looked. There were outlines of footprints in the dust on the sill. You would expect to find something on the sill, probably footprints. But you might not expect to find these particular footprints. The funny thing about these was that there were only two prints. One pointing out and one in. Both of them were small and both had been made by bare feet—or, more truly, by one bare foot, the right one. Unless they had been made by a very dainty guy, they were a woman's footprints.

"What do you know?" I said to myself. "Looks like she was killed by a one-legged woman."

I went to the foot of the bed and bent over and stared at the bottoms of Miss Mason's dead feet. They were as clean as you'd want them. Not a smudge. Not a dust streak anywhere.

There was a dressing gown, a filmy, pink and white business, lying across the footboard of the bed. On the bed, part of it crumpled under Miss Mason's feet, lay a blue nightgown. On the floor beside the bed was a pair of blue slippers with white puffs on the toes, and a pair of bath slippers, wooden soles with straps. There was no other clothing in sight. A wardrobe trunk stood in a corner of the room. The closet door beside the dresser was closed. I opened it and glanced inside. There were dresses and things hanging up, neat and undisturbed, and on the door hung a clean white laundry bag.

"A neat lady," I thought. "Stuff she had been wearing put away. Place for everything. Nothing lying around."

I closed the door and looked over the dresser. There was toilet stuff, mirror, comb, brush, boxes of powder and some bottles of perfume, nail polish, toilet water, and one thing and another. These were all neat and clean. Also on the dresser was a candy box. It had been used for candy once, but now it contained cookies, small chocolate cookies with bits of nuts in them. There were maybe a dozen left. They were homemade cookies and they smelled wonderful. I reached for one, then stopped.

Like stealing the pennies from a dead man's eyes, I thought.

There was nothing else on the dresser except some marks. Here's where she wasn't quite neat. There were some rings on the dresser scarf that would have been made by wet glasses. There were quite a few rings, all interlocking. You couldn't tell whether there had been one glass or two or three. I touched the stains. They were still damp. I glanced into the closet again and around the room, but there were no glasses in sight.

I took a last look at Marian Mason's body. I was surprised that there was such a little bit of blood. But I didn't get any ideas looking at her, so I went out of the room and downstairs.

In the lobby things had quieted down. Most of the people were gone. Pete stood over by Harry Baird's desk, still mopping his neck but looking less red in the face. I said nothing to him, but stepped into the sitting room of the suite and closed the door behind me. I looked at the litter on Singer's desk and stopped. He'd only been in bed a couple of hours. It was damned hard to get him there, and now I was thinking of waking him up again.

Maybe, I thought, it could wait till the county attorney showed up. Give him another hour's sleep.

No, I thought. It is at times like these that Joe Spinder needs the wisdom of Singer Batts. Because, to be frank, I don't think that county attorney is going to be able to figure this thing out. And I think maybe Singer Batts will.

So, asleep or not, I thought, he's got to get up and think it over.

I stepped over to Singer's bedroom and opened the door quietly. I looked into the room. The bed was as neat as a pin. Hadn't even been opened. Singer was sitting in his old Boston rocker by the window, fully dressed. He smiled at me as I came in.

"What is it, Joe?" he said.

"What's what?"

"What's the trouble?"

"You never went to bed at all," I said.

"No. I've been waiting."

"Waiting! To find out what the trouble is?"

"Yes, Joe."

"But there wasn't any trouble when you started to go to bed."

Singer just smiled.

"How'd you know?" I said. "Who tipped you off?"

"Nobody," Singer said. "It was clear that something was on your mind. I thought that sooner or later you'd come and tell me."

"But this is something different."

He stopped smiling. "Yes?"

"We've got a murder on our hands."

His voice was a whisper. "A murder, Joe?"

I saw that old look come into his eyes and I began to get scared.

"Who?" he asked.

"Marian Mason."

"Who is Marian Mason?"

"Marian Mason has been living in this hotel for about two weeks. She came to town last fall. She is a schoolteacher and a very luscious dish."

"Did the murder take place in the hotel?"

"Yeah. In the hotel. I have seen her corpse with my own eyes."

"Well, Joe," he said, settling himself in his chair, "you know how to handle these things better than I. You've called the District Attorney?"

"Mr. Rowe called him around twelve noon."

"Well, I imagine they'll have it straightened out in no time."

He looked out the window.

So now I could see it. We were going to have to play that game again. I took off my coat and sat down on the edge of the bed.

"Now listen, Singer," I said. "You know that phony from Montpelier won't be able to figure this thing out. He'll just try to pin it on somebody and maybe he can make it stick and maybe not."

Singer was still gazing out the window. "Well?" he said.

"Well, then, somebody's got to really figure it out."

"Whom do you suggest?"

"You," I said.

"I thought so."

I heaved a sigh of relief.

"Okay," I said. "We've got that far."

"No, Joe," Singer said. "I can't undertake it."

"Why?" I said. "You figured out who killed Abel Morris on his farm two years ago. You figured out that double murder in Montpelier—the man and wife that died in their car. You figured out who robbed Harry Oats's jewelry store and killed the cop on the road to Detroit. No cops could figure those out. You did."

"But I was pushed into those cases, Joe. I didn't want to. I'm a theorist—not a detective. I'm a scholar. I do it out of books."

"So," I said. "Now you've got a real-life case. Right in your lap."

"But I don't like real-life cases. I hate murder."

"Who doesn't?" I said.

Singer shivered. "No, Joe. Really, I'm not up to it. You handle it."

I looked at him. "Oh sure. Me. I'll handle it. I'm just the best little detective there is."

"Don't be bitter, Joe. It's just that I—"

"All right," I said. "Forget it."

I tried to look hurt as I put my coat on and picked up my hat.

It's a funny thing about Singer Batts. He's not a coward. You can't scare him with a gun. I've seen him stand up to gorillas twice his size without batting an eye. But when it comes to murder, he shrinks from it like a cat from water. He just doesn't like to mess around with it. Once he gets started, he goes through with it. You can't drag him away. But he certainly hates to get started.

When I opened the door Singer said, "I'm sorry, Joe."

"That's all right," I said. "The hell with it."

I dropped my hat on the desk in the sitting room and went back to the hotel lobby.

There was quite a gang out there now. Most of it was hanging around Pete Haley. Pete was sweating and rubbing his big red neck with the bandanna, trying to answer all the questions without committing himself. There was another gang around Harry Baird. He was getting grumpy. He kept waving toward Pete Haley. It was a dirty trick. Pete had all he could do. But Harry was red in the face and disgusted and wouldn't say anything. Then there was a third little gang, mostly women, gathered around one of the old davenports near the big east window, listening to Nancy Wheeler. Nancy was having a hard time telling the story. She would talk a little, then half-scream, remembering, then cry a little and wipe her eyes, and then talk again, faster and louder than ever.

"So I went right ahead," she was saying, "not knowing a thing, and opened the door, like I always do, to get in there and clean the room, and then I dropped my duster and them clean sheets and all right on the floor. Because there she was, in broad daylight, laying there on the bed, stark nekkid, a big knife sticking in her chest, and blood all over everything. My land, I tell you—" and Nancy broke down again and the women gasped and looked at each other, shaking their heads, clucking and making out that it was the most awful thing they ever heard. But you could tell most of them were lapping it up.

I went up to Pete.

"Did Mr. Rowe call the D.A.?" I said.

"Yes," Pete said. "He's comin' right over. Mr. Rowe went back to the bank."

"All right. Get these people out of here. Harry will help."

Pete gave me a desperate look but he began to move the people out. I got hold of Harry Baird.

"Help Pete clear this lobby," I said, "and send Nancy Wheeler home. Then go down to the tavern and get me two quarts of bourbon."

Harry blinked. Then he opened his eyes wide.

"Oh," he said. "It's like that?"

"It's like that," I said.

Harry moved away.

As I turned from the desk, Curly Evans came into the lobby from the stairs, swung up to the desk in his big, muscle-bound way and threw his key to me.

"Up kind of late, aren't you?" I said.

"My day off," Curly said, and started away. He had a big bundle of laundry under his arm. Pete caught sight of him and came over.

"Your room on the second floor, Curly?" Pete said.

"Yeah," said Curly, looking straight at Pete. "What about it?"

"East side, or west side?"

"East side."

"Back?"

"That's right."

"You in it all night?"

"What's it to you?"

Pete was a little embarrassed. He'd started out to play detective and then lost his nerve.

"Oh, nothin', I was just wonderin'," he said.

Curly started off again.

"Oh, Curly," Pete said.

"Yeah?"

"You be around later?"

"Maybe."

"You better drop in around noon. Man here may want to talk to you."

"Yeah?"

Curly looked at Pete a moment and then went out, the bundle tight under his arm, letting the door slam behind him.

Harry came up then.

"Curly's a pretty tough boy," Harry said.

"Hmn," said Pete.

"One mornin'," Harry said, "Nancy was cleanin' up and she found Curly's sheet covered with blood. She come runnin' down here and made a fuss, and when Curly come in that night I asked him about it. ''Twasn't nothin',' he said. 'Had a smashed fingernail, kept me awake. I took a knife I had up there and cut the damn thing off.'"

"Curly ever give you any real trouble?" Pete asked.

"Never. Curly is a nice, quiet boy."

I grinned at that, thinking of the stories I'd heard about Curly. He'd go up to the City and set a whole jointful of the toughest mugs in town by the ears. But I guess that around Preston he was a quiet boy.

"You'd better get Jack Pritchard over here, too," I said.

"He won't like it," Harry said.

"So what? Did you get that liquor?"

"Here."

I took the two bottles.

"When the county law comes," I said, "cooperate with them, but don't go out of your way. I'm going back to the suite. If they want to see me, call me on the phone first."

I went into the sitting room. I opened one of the bottles and got out two glasses. I rang for Dora and told her to get some ice cubes out and be ready to bring them in fast when I rang again. Then I sat down at the desk and got out some paper.

I began to write down everything that had happened from the time Pete brought those kids in early in the morning to the time I left Harry and Pete at the desk a few minutes before. I drew a little diagram of the murder room and listed everything I could remember seeing.

This was a tough job and I was only halfway through it at one o'clock when there was a knock on the door.

"Come in," I said.

It was Harry Baird.

"The District Attorney's here," he said.

"Weaver?"

Harry nodded.

"He bring a gang with him?"

"Four guys."

"You take him up to Miss Mason's room?"

"Yes."

"You call Jack Pritchard?"

"I did. He said he'd be over."

"All right. Go back to the desk and keep your eyes open."

Harry closed the door. I went back to my job.

* * * *

The house phone on my desk rang. I picked it up. It was Harry.

"The District Attorney would like to see you now," he said.

"Stall for about three minutes and send him in," I said. "Don't hang up yet. Pretend you're still talking to me."

I laid the phone down, picked up my story of recent events, the bottle of whisky and a bottle of mix, and rang for Dora. I went into Singer's room. He was still sitting in his chair by the window reading one of his ancient books. I threw my papers into his lap.

"Here," I said. "I wrote it all out for you. Now you got it in a book. Who killed the beautiful schoolteacher? And if you get interested—" Dora came in with a bowl of ice. I dropped some in Singer's glass. "If you get interested, here's something to wash it down with."

Singer was shaking his head.

"No. It won't work, Joe. I don't want to get into—"

"All right," I said. "Forget it."

But I left the stuff with him and when I went out I didn't close his door all the way. I left it open a crack.

The whisky was in case Singer got interested. He hated to get started on a murder case so much that he needed the liquor to bolster him up. It was the only time he ever drank. Then he really put it away. Still, I've never seen him drunk.

I took the bowl of ice back to the desk, put some in my glass and was mixing my drink when the door opened and four men came in. One of them was in uniform. Two were plain-clothes men and the fourth was the District Attorney—Gerald Weaver.

"Well, well," I said. "The whole county government. Will somebody have a drink?"

The two plain-clothes men looked at Weaver. He shook his head and they looked at the bottle and shook their heads, too—slowly.

"Your name Joe Spinder?" Weaver asked.

"Yeah."

"I want to ask you a few questions."

"Sure," I said. "But don't be nasty about it. You're a guest in this hotel."

"I won't be here long," he said.

"That's good."

Weaver was a pompous little guy with a pot belly and pig eyes. I'd run into him a year before when Singer figured out for him who killed the man and wife in Montpelier. I hadn't liked Weaver then and I didn't like him now. Of course, I've got an ingrown prejudice against cops. Years of hobo-ing made me pretty sour.

"Sit down," I said.

"You watch the door." Weaver motioned to the uniformed cop, who set his back against the door to the lobby.

Weaver sat down in the leather chair by the window near Singer's work table. The two dicks sat on the love seat on the other side of the table. They were all staring at me.

"What is this?" I asked.

"How long have you lived in Preston?" asked Weaver.

"Five years."

"Been running this hotel all the time?"

"Yeah."

"How'd you happen to come here?"

"I drifted in one day and it looked like a nice little place to settle down."

"What were you doing before you came here?"

"Just traveling," I said.

"Just a bum, eh? You spent your first night here in jail, didn't you?"

I set my drink down on the desk and looked him over.

"Oh," I said. "It's going to be like that. Okay, I'm through. I'm willing to cooperate—to help solve the crime. But no goddam two-penny cop is going to push me around. You can stay out of my life and go on about your business."

One of the dicks got up from the love seat, walked across the room and slugged me with the back of his hand. My chair tipped sideways and I got up and let it fall.

"Why, you dirty bastard!"

Just as I went for him he backed away, and Weaver said:

"Come back and sit down, Olson. We won't have any trouble with this guy."

"The hell you won't." I picked up my chair and sat down again. "You're pretty cocky," I said. "You talk like you've got this thing all figured out."

"I think I have."

"Yeah? Who killed her?"

"You."

I took a long drink.

"You are nuts," I said.

"Am I?" He leered at me. "Tell me—when did you and this Mason woman plan to get married?"

I could only stare at him.

"Well?"

"My God!" I said.

"Answer the question," Weaver snapped, pulling a paper out of his pocket. "When did you plan to get married?"

"You're all wrong," I said. "We've been married eighteen years. I met her in London back in the spring of 'ninety-eight. We went to Niagara Falls and then to Paris. Spent five years in Darkest Africa. I was looking for Livingstone at the time."

"Very funny. Maybe you won't feel so funny when you see this evidence. It's a marriage license, made out in Montpelier for Marian Mason and Joe Spinder. Dated yesterday."

"Where did you find it?"

"In the top bureau drawer in the dead girl's room."

I thought it over. "So I killed her?"

"I think you did," Weaver said.

"So I was going to marry her in a couple of days and so I killed her."

Olson got up again. I was so sore I couldn't see straight. I poured out half a glass of bourbon and started to drink it neat.

"Why, you cheap half-baked lousy goddam two-faced pimply politician," I said, "you haven't got the sense of a pigeon. That is so ridiculous it stinks from here to Hollywood. I wouldn't answer any more stupid questions for you if my life depended on it. And to start things off, you can get the hell out of here."

Olson was standing by my chair.

"You keep your eye on him, Olson," Weaver said. "Now then, when did you get home last night?"

"Get out of here," I said. "Scram. Beat it, or I'll fix it so you won't have a job the rest of your life."

"I should think," he said, "that a man under suspicion, as you are, would be more careful—"

"Who's under suspicion?"

Weaver was losing his temper, too.

"You killed Marian Mason."

"Like hell I did."

"Now you listen to me—"

And then suddenly there was a new voice, saying, "Gentlemen. Gentlemen, let's be sensible about this thing."

I looked. It was Singer Batts, standing in the doorway of his room, surveying us. In one hand he held the sheaf of papers I'd given him, and in the other, a drink. I could hear the ice tinkling in the glass. And when I saw that glass and heard that ice tinkling, I knew that from now on everything would be all right.

CHAPTER 4

Everybody was staring at Singer. Weaver was the first one to speak and all he said was, "Oh. It's you."

He remembered all right. A guy never likes somebody who does the work he gets the credit for, and Weaver took the credit in Montpelier for solving the crime that Singer really solved.

"I couldn't help overhearing you," Singer said. "It seems to me you were making some rather hasty assumptions."

"Does it? I think I have plenty of reason to arrest Spinder, here, for murder."

"Have you established the fact of murder?" Singer asked. "Have you held an inquest?"

"We'll hold an inquest. Don't worry. But that doesn't have any bearing on my suspicions of Spinder."

"I'm afraid you'd have a hard time building up a court case against Spinder."

"Just what makes you think so?"

Singer lifted the papers I'd given him a few minutes before.

"I have here a complete record of certain events that have occurred in and around this hotel during the last ten hours."

"How do you happen to have such a record?" Weaver asked, suspicious, his little pig eyes half closed.

In his quiet, easy way Singer said, "I am the owner of this hotel. I live in it. I have a certain interest in what takes place under my own roof. When a murder is committed in the hotel, I think I am within my rights in conducting an investigation." That didn't go down well with Weaver at all.

"So you're going to play detective again."

Singer smiled.

"Perhaps. I had determined to have nothing to do with this murder beyond cooperating with the law as a private citizen. I told Joe Spinder that I would not inject myself into it in any way. But I changed my mind."

"Why?"

"When I heard you making extravagant and ridiculous charges against Joe Spinder, I could no longer help myself. I was bound to come to Joe's defense." Weaver was running out of sarcasm and beginning to think it over.

"You have some reason," he said, "to think Spinder is innocent?"

"I have every reason to think he is innocent and none whatever to think he is guilty. This report contains a good deal of food for thought. It suggests several lines of reasoning—all of which are extremely interesting and none of which points, even by the wildest stretch of the imagination, to Joe Spinder."

Weaver sat down. "Let me see that report."

Singer smiled again.

"Ah, no, Mr. Weaver. This is a confidential report, made for me alone. It contains information of a private nature which has no bearing on the murder."

"You're withholding evidence," Weaver said. "A serious offense. Give me the report."

Singer's voice sharpened.

"I shall be glad to tell you all the facts I know that bear on the case," he said. "But I will not give you this report, as written, and you know as well as I that I am not legally bound to."

Weaver gave up. "All right. Tell me the facts." Singer looked around the room.

"The place has the air of a prison. Please ask your ruffians to leave."

The bruisers on the love seat began to pout. Weaver couldn't make up his mind. So nobody moved. Singer shambled, stoop-shouldered and thin, across the room and opened the door. There was a dead pause for a full minute. Then Weaver's head dropped forward. The two dicks got up and walked out and the cop in uniform followed them. Singer closed the door and turned back to Weaver.

"Well," Weaver said, "now that you've fixed it up the way you want it, let's have those facts you were talking about. Then I can go about my business."

"It won't take long," Singer said. "Joe will correct me if I'm wrong...

"At two-forty-five this morning our local constable brought two boys to the hotel and asked Joe to put them up for the night. They had been out on the street, carousing and Pete—our village policeman—didn't want to put them in jail."

"That's what jails are for," Weaver said.

Singer smiled.

"Of course," he said. "Joe agreed and he and Pete took the boys upstairs and put them to bed."

It was right about in here that I began to hear the strange sound. I'm pretty sensitive to any kind of noise in the hotel, and especially to unusual ones. It's my job.

I knew all about what Singer was telling Weaver and I knew he wouldn't make any mistakes. So I gave my attention to these noises.

They were faint and far away. I don't think Singer and Weaver heard them. They came from underneath us, from the cellar under the hotel. I could tell they were coming from the old section of the cellar that we didn't use any more. The furnace and storeroom were on the other side of the building. That's why the sounds were unusual. There wasn't any reason for anybody or anything to be down there.

It sounded like somebody hauling stuff across the floor. There would be a long, slow, faint scraping sound. Then it would stop, and after a minute there would be another. Then some dull thuds—very faint.

I listened. It got under my skin and I got up and went to the door.

"Excuse me," I said to Singer, "you're doing all right."

"Just a minute," Weaver said. "Where are you going?"

"I thought I'd go play a little bridge with your three stooges," I said.

"You're under suspicion, Spinder," Weaver said. "I'm forced to restrict your movements until the suspicions have been cleared up."

"Come now, Mr. Weaver," said Singer. "You have men to guard the hotel. I give you my assurance that Joe will not try to make his escape. The management of a hotel entails constant vigilance. You surely will permit us to keep our business running."

Weaver tried to argue, but couldn't. Singer didn't leave him any room. Finally Weaver said, "Well—don't leave the hotel."

"Thank you," I said.

I went out to the lobby.

Weaver's three stooges were gathered around the desk, throwing questions at Harry Baird. Harry kept trying to go to sleep. But they wouldn't let him. They all looked at me when I came through the door, but nobody said anything.

I went back to the kitchen and through the kitchen to the shed at the back end of the building where the cellar door was. Just inside the cellar door I pushed back a section in the stair rail and hauled out my flashlight. I keep it in that hiding place so I'll always have it when I need it.

At the bottom of the steps on the east side of the building was the furnace room and coal bin. On the west side was a storage room. These rooms had been floored, and finished off with plaster. But beyond them toward the front of the building it was all just excavation, some pilings, and stone walls and dirt floor, with planks here and there where it was a little damp. Every once in a while there would be a narrow little window just above the ground level. But the windows were too dirty to let any light in. The place was a regular dungeon.

I had heard the sounds again when I went down the steps and as I passed the boiler room, but when I stepped into the old section of the cellar and flashed my light around they stopped. My flashlight wouldn't reach to the far corners of the big chamber, so I started across a piece of planking toward the front.

Something swished past my face and I ducked and lost my balance and stepped off the plank into mud. I had the hell scared out of me and my heart was pounding like a punch press when I got back on the plank. I flashed my light around the walls near me and then began to breathe easier.

"Goddam," I said aloud. "Bats. Bats in the basement." I laughed.

My voice sounded hollow and silly down there, so I stopped making comments and began to move again. After a few steps I ran out of plank. I stood on the end of it, wondering whether it was worthwhile to go any farther and poking around with my light, and suddenly I heard something, different from the first sounds I'd heard—a sort of clomp-clomp, like somebody walking in the mud. It seemed to come from my right and a little behind me.

I jerked around with the flash and after a moment I pinned it down. It was somebody all right and he was heading back for the passage between the furnace room and the storeroom.

He was in mud and I had a plank to walk on, so I beat him to it. I reached out, grabbed collar and hung on. I flashed the light in his face.

It was Roy Blake.

He was a sight. His clothes were wrinkled and muddy. His pants legs were solid mud to the knees. His face was streaked with it and his eyes stared out of it like two white saucers. He was scared to death and his lips were shaking. I eased up on my grip and he stumbled back and leaned against one of the pilings.

"Well, well," I said. "What are you looking for—gold?"

He didn't say anything, just lifted his arm and pointed vaguely and let his arm drop. I looked over in the corner where he'd pointed.

Piled up on the ground was a bunch of old boxes, crates, and junk of one kind and another, and up on top of them was one of the planks from the floor, angled up from the pile of junk to the ledge of one of those little windows. Leaning against the pile was another plank that I guess he hadn't got clear up yet.

I looked at him.

"You were trying to get out through that window?" I said.

He nodded his head.

"Why, boy," I said, "you could never have got that window open. Those windows weren't made to open."

"I could have broke it," he said in a trembling little voice.

"But why? You didn't have any reason to sneak out of this hotel."

"I wasn't sneaking out. I was hiding. I didn't want to get caught on the street. I was going to wait for night. I was going away."

"What have you two kids got into?" I said. "Where did your pal, Granger, go?"

"I don't know."

"Why didn't you go with him?"

"I didn't think we ought to—then. But he went any way. Then I didn't want to take the rap alone."

"The rap? for what? What'd you do? Kill somebody?"

He shivered all over and tried to wipe some of the mud off his face with his sleeve. He only made it worse.

"No," he said. "We didn't. We didn't kill—anybody. Honest. Look," he said, "you help me out of here, will you? I'll go right home. Honest to God I will."

I was beginning to see a little light.

"You went prowling around that schoolteacher's room last night, didn't you?"

He didn't answer that. He just said, "We didn't kill her. Honest to God."

"So she was dead when you saw her."

"Yes," he said.

"Did you go in her room?"

"No. We just looked in through the window."

"Was the shade up?"

"Yeah."

"You didn't go in?"

"No."

"How did you know she was dead?"

"By the way she was lying there. And we could see the knife."

"So you were afraid somebody might think you did it, so you decided to lam out."

"Harley did. I said we ought to tell Pete Haley and stay here. Then when he went anyway and I was alone, I got scared."

I thought it over.

"But how did you get your clothes?" I said.

He didn't answer.

"Somebody had to help you. Who was it?"

He still wouldn't answer.

"Was it Jack Pritchard?"

He shook his head.

Then all of a sudden there was somebody standing over me and a voice said: "Well, well, well. Two little Boy Scouts."

I looked up. It was Olson, Weaver's bruiser, and right behind him was his brother officer. Olson grabbed Roy Blake and pulled him up tight.

"Who's the kid?" he said.

"Go peddle your papers," I said. "He's not the killer."

"I'll come to you in a minute, bum," Olson said. "Stew, take the kid upstairs. I want to have a little talk with Mr. Spinder."

"Okay," the other dick said. "Come on, punk."

He took Roy Blake's arm and pulled him away.

The kid threw me a look.

"Go ahead," I told him. "They're cops, but don't tell 'em anything. They'll twist it."

Olson wiped the back of his hand across my mouth, hard.

"Shut up, you."

The footsteps died away. Olson grabbed the flashlight out of my hand and flashed it on my face. "Now. We're all alone. Nobody to bother us."

"All right. What do you want? A confession?"

"That's it."

"Get out your paper and pencil."

He laughed—if you could call it laughing. "Oh, no. It ain't that simple. Anyway, I'd need witnesses."

"Okay. Let's go upstairs. I'll give you the whole story."

"Ain't you smart? 'Let's go upstairs.' Not yet, bum. I'm just going to get you in shape for it."

"You want me to hold the light?"

I was just showing off. I didn't feel that good, really. That big hunk of beef could make jelly out of me if I wasn't lucky, and I didn't expect to be lucky. He was at least six feet two and must have weighed two-fifty. I'm not over five-ten and I never weighed more than one-sixty.

"You slug me just once," I said, "and I'll make life hell for you."

He laughed again. And slugged me. Pain shot through my head and I blinked. He came boring in with his left hand, giving it to me twice before I could gather myself together. He was holding the flashlight with his right hand.

I ducked under his arm as he started another one and slammed my fist down onto his right wrist. The flashlight fell out of his hand onto the ground. It didn't go out, but it didn't throw much of a light on me, either.

I straightened up and hit him in the belly with my right and tried to cross a left, but he stopped that one and hung one on my head again. My head was splitting by this time and I kept seeing flashes of blue and green. He hit me again with that left and I fell backward, slamming my head against the plank and rolling off into the mud.

He waited for me to get up. I took my time about it, trying to clear my head, to get the knifelike pains out of it. My face felt twice as big as normal.

I got to my knees and he started for me again, but I pulled my legs up under me and dived under his arms into his thighs. He went over my back. One of his feet caught me in the side of the head. I heard him flop into the mud and I got up and turned around. I had a clear road out of the cellar and I could have made a break and got upstairs, but I was sore and now that I'd got him down once I felt better about my chances.

I let him get up to his hands and knees and then I walked up close and kicked him in the chest. But I was too cocky. He grabbed my foot and hauled up on it and I went flat on my back, banging my head again on the plank. Then he was all over me. He held me down with one knee on my chest and started pounding.

I felt sick and cold. His big hands kept smacking my head from side to side. His knee was squeezing the wind out of me. I felt so damned helpless.

Then I heard voices and saw a light coming. I opened my mouth and let out the loudest yell I could manage. The big dick lifted his arm over his head and started down. But it never landed. I heard Weaver's voice saying, "Olson!" and slowly the big gorilla climbed off me and stood up.

I picked up my flashlight, which was still burning, and got up, trying to brush some of the mud off my clothes. I flashed the light on Olson, then on Weaver. Behind Weaver I saw Singer Batts.

Olson looked a little sheepish and Weaver looked worried.

"Hello," I said.

After a moment Singer said to Weaver: "I don't think Mr. Olson will be working for this county much longer. I'll thank you now to remove him from this hotel, and, better still, from this town. Right away."

I had never heard Singer lay it on the line like that before. It sounded pretty good. I grinned. It made my mouth feel like it was splitting.

"I'll see that Olson is taken care of," Weaver said. "You needn't bother to file charges."

I looked at Olson, then at Weaver.

"What's he got on you?" I asked.

Olson made a growling sound in his throat and headed my way again, but Weaver grabbed his arm.

"Go out to the car," Weaver said, "and stay there."

Olson walked away.

Singer beckoned to me. "You'd better come upstairs and take a shower."

We started off; then Singer turned back to Weaver, who hadn't moved.

"If you want to look around the cellar for evidence," Singer said, "you're welcome."

I looked back at Weaver.

"Am I still under suspicion?" I asked.

After a moment, Weaver said, "Certainly."

Beside me, Singer was laughing softly.

"It's funny?" I said.

"Mr. Weaver is amusing in his stubbornness."

"Yeah," I said. "Isn't he?"

We went on upstairs and into the suite through the kitchen. I took off my clothes and went into the bathroom to clean up.

CHAPTER 5

When I came out of the shower and got some clean clothes on and a couple of patches on the cuts on my face I felt better. I went over and poured a drink.

Singer had pulled his rocker in from the bedroom and was sitting over by his table, his feet up on the love seat, the bottle of whisky on the table beside him—it was half gone, I noticed—and a lot of papers spread out. He was opening his mail, and I could see that he was looking for something special. He'd pick up an envelope, look at it, and throw it onto the table. Finally I heard him give a little chortle and open one up. He was excited, for Singer, and I watched him.

He pulled a letter from the envelope and opened it carefully, taking something out. He squirmed around in his seat and held the something up to the light. It was a photograph.

Oh, Lord—no! I thought. Not that again.

"What did they learn from the Blake kid?" I said, trying to get him started on something about the crime.

"Hmn?" Singer said.

"The Blake kid," I said. "What did they learn from him?"

He didn't answer at all this time. I resigned myself. After a minute or two he looked over at me and said, in an uncertain little voice, "Joe."

"All right," I said, and got up.

I went over and stood behind his chair, looking over his shoulder. The photograph was the picture of a woman, maybe thirty years old, maybe forty. She wore glasses, and she had a snub nose and practically no chin. You could see that the photo had been retouched for all it was worth. In Singer's lap lay the letter. It was written on blue paper under a flourishing letterhead: "The Belleforest Lonely Hearts Society—Every man needs a good wife; every woman a fine husband."

"Singer."

He looked at me like a little kid caught in the cookie jar.

"I thought you gave this up a long time ago."

"But, Joe," he said, "a man ought to have a wife. A man is only a shell without a wife. A man needs a home—a real—"

"That's not the way to get a wife," I said. "This town is full of women who would jump at the chance to hook up with you. Why don't you look around?"

"Well, Joe, to be absolutely honest with you, I have yet to see in Preston a young woman whose intelligence is attractive to me."

"You don't marry an intelligence," I said. "You marry a woman. And you don't marry a woman with a face like that." I pointed to the photograph.

"But beauty is only skin deep," Singer said.

"It's more than skin deep on that mug," I said.

"Don't be vulgar, Joe."

I laughed. "Look who's saying 'Don't be vulgar.' The Belleforest Lonely Hearts Society. For Christ's sake!"

He looked hurt. I guess I shouldn't be so hard on him. This correspondence with lonely hearts clubs is Singer's only vice—and I suppose it isn't exactly a vice either. But I never could figure it out in him. About everything else he was smart. But he would keep on looking for a wife by mail. I think the true reason was that he was afraid to associate with real, living women and would never be able to bring himself to ask anybody to marry him.

He laid the photograph and letter on his table.

"I'm sorry," I said. "You're not vulgar. I know it. I hope you find a wife."

"Maybe—someday—" he said.

He mixed himself another drink. That made me feel good because it showed me that he had started to think about the murder again.

I went back to my chair and picked up my own drink.

"They didn't learn anything from young Blake," he said.

"How'd you happen to come down cellar and find us?"

"The other detective came upstairs and brought young Blake in here. He told us that he had left you and Olson downstairs. I couldn't imagine what you and Olson would have in common, so I insisted we go down and investigate."

"I'm glad. That bastard would have killed me."

"I have no doubt of it."

There was a pause. Then Singer went on, "I have made up my mind that we will investigate the death of Miss Marian Mason."

"Good," I said. "Where do we start?"

"We start in the only possible way. We start with certain assumptions. We assume that Marian Mason was killed by somebody in this town. We assume she was killed by someone who had known her for a certain length of time—a week, a month, three months. Of course, these assumptions may be incorrect. But they will do to start with, because we don't have any better ones. And in line with these assumptions, Joe, our first step is to start checking on the history of Miss Mason in this town. It may be an interesting search. Because Marian Mason was a very beautiful girl, and the history of a beautiful girl is likely to be more interesting than the history of a girl who is not beautiful. Not always, mind you, but sometimes."

"That sounds wonderful. What, actually, do we do?"

"We build the history of Marian Mason, out of everything we can find about her. I want to start with you. Tell me about her. How long had she been living in the hotel?"

"About ten days," I said. "Before that, she was living with Mrs. Fogarty. I don't know why she moved. In a town like Preston she wouldn't have much more private life in a hotel than she would anywhere else."

"Is there anything you can think of that might have driven her out of the Fogarty home?"

"No. She went around with Bill Fogarty for a while, just after she came here last fall. But Bill's been in the army since before Christmas. She stayed on for six months."

"What other romantic interests did she have in Preston?"

"She went around with Tommy Rowe and Don Eastman."

"Both at once?"

"Well, the three of them were together a lot. Tommy was her real boyfriend. I think Eastman just went along for the ride. Or maybe he had a girl in some other town."

"Eastman—he lives in the hotel, doesn't he?"

"He does. On the same floor where Miss Mason used to live."

"Didn't Eastman ever go out with local girls?"

"Sometimes," I said. "He's been known to run around some with Elsie Schaffner."

"Who is Elsie Schaffner?"

"She's a very sweet little girl, lovely to look at. Her father owns the filling station down at the end of town near the bridge. She's in high school."

"How old is Eastman?"

I shrugged. "Twenty-eight—thirty maybe."

"How old would you say Tommy Rowe is?"

"He looks forty," I said, "but he's under thirty really."

"Would you say, in general, that Miss Mason was a bad girl?"

"I wouldn't say," I said, "because I don't say things like that. The School Board didn't think she was so good. I know they didn't renew her contract."

"Wasn't she a good teacher?"

"She was a good teacher, I guess. But you know how it is in a little town. She smoked, she was always running off to the City with Tommy

Rowe, she never went to church. They expect a schoolteacher to be a gilded angel."

"Then Miss Mason was no gilded angel, I take it."

"What are you trying to do, trap me?" I said. "I don't claim she was a gilded angel."

"That's very chivalrous of you, Joe."

"Nuts," I said.

"Did you ever know her before she came to Preston?"

"No. Of course not."

"You don't know of any jealousies revolving around her, jealousies that might have furnished a motive for murder?"

"No. Bill Fogarty probably didn't like it when she took up with Tommy Rowe. But Bill wouldn't kill her."

"He wouldn't?"

"I don't think so."

"Has Bill Fogarty been home on leave lately?"

"Yeah, he came home a couple of weeks ago. Just went back last night."

"Was he seen with Miss Mason at that time?"

"I don't know. I never saw him with her."

There was a noise like thunder on the stairs outside. The door of the sitting room flew open and Harry Baird came in. He was panting, and red in the face again, and you could see that he was getting sore at somebody. "What's up?" I said.

"My God," said Harry Baird, "you'd think I committed some crime myself. He wants that salesman, the one checked out of here five-thirty this mornin'. He claims he's got the case all figured. He tells me to get hold of that guy's address in Detroit so's he can have him picked up."

"Mr. Weaver thinks a traveling salesman did it?" Singer said.

Harry snorted.

"Got it all figured out. Crime of passion. Guy got up in the night, busted into Miss Mason's room, got rejected, and flew off the handle. Killed her."

"With a butcher knife," Singer said.

"Sounds goofy, don't it?" Harry said. "Funny thing is, though, this guy sold butcher knives. All kinds of cutlery. That was his line. He showed me last night when he come in. Had two sample cases full of knives."

"Do you know whether he made any sales?" I said.

"Yeah, he told me he made some. Took quite a big order at the hardware store. Sold the bakery two of 'em. Delivered those two right on the spot."

"The bakery?" I said, and looked at Singer.

"What about the bakery?" Singer said.

"Don Eastman works at the bakery."

"Is that so?"

"Is Eastman up yet?" I said to Harry.

Harry looked uncomfortable. "Well, yes. He's up. But he ain't here."

"He's not here?"

"Nope. He ain't anywhere around. The D.A. was looking for him just a few minutes ago. Nobody saw him leave. He's just gone."

"Maybe he just went to work."

Harry shook his head.

"Nope, he didn't. Because Mrs. Coolidge called up from the bakery a while back and asked whether he was sick. He hadn't showed up yet."

"Well, well," Singer said softly.

"Anything else going on out there?" I said.

"Not much. Weaver's got Doc Blane examining the corpse."

"Doc Blane?" Singer said. "Doesn't he have his own medical man?"

"The county examiner got held up. He'll be along later," Harry answered.

I got up.

"Harry," I said, "will you send my suit over to the cleaner's?"

I picked the suit up from the desk and, out of habit, looked through the pockets. In the coat pocket I found the envelope Tommy Rowe had given me to put in Marian Mason's box. I'd forgotten all about it.

I laid the envelope on the desk and handed the suit to Harry. He took it and started to back out the door.

"Oh, Harry," Singer said, "will you ask Doc Blane to stop in here when he comes down?"

"Sure." He went out and I picked up the envelope.

"This I forgot about," I said.

"What is it?" Singer said.

"Tommy Rowe gave it to me to put in Marian Mason's box. When I went to the bank."

Singer's fingers began to twitch.

"Better give it back to Tommy?" I said.

After a moment Singer said, "Is it sealed?"

"Very little," I said.

I looked at the envelope. Marian Mason's name was scrawled across it. There was nothing else on it.

"It may be vital evidence," I said.

Singer's lingers were twitching like fury.

"I shouldn't like to give it to the District Attorney," he said.

"No," I said.

"On the other hand, as you say—Open it, Joe, for goodness' sake."

I pulled up the flap and drew out the contents of the envelope. It opened easily. He must have sealed it in a hurry. It was just barely stuck.

There was a sheet of plain white paper folded over something. I unfolded the paper and a bunch of money fell out. I picked up the money and counted it. There were ten bright new hundred-dollar bills.

"A thousand bucks," I said to Singer.

"Anything in writing?" he said.

"Yeah." I read the note written on the plain sheet of paper. "*I don't think you got anything out of Father. This is all I can get together now. Please be patient. All my love, Tommy.*"

Singer made a bad face.

"Don't worry about it," I said. "He'll never know. I'll put it back in here and give it to him. He'll never know."

"Nevertheless," Singer said, "it isn't quite fair."

There was a tap at the door.

"Come in," I said.

The door opened and Doc Blane came in. The Doc was a nice old gentleman with snow-white hair, a thin, red little face, and the quietest voice in the world. He wore black string ties and stiff collars.

He came in, bowing at both of us, and sat down by my desk.

"Pretty gruesome business, Doctor," Singer said.

Doc Blane sighed.

"A shame," he said. "A lovely girl."

"When did it happen?" Singer asked.

Doc shook his head and laughed softly.

"I'm just a country practitioner—no police experience. I can only guess."

"What would you guess?" said Singer.

"Well, I guessed for the District Attorney that she'd been dead for at least fifteen hours."

"About midnight last night," Singer said.

"Yes. But I could be wrong as much as three hours either way."

"Nancy Wheeler," Singer said, "claimed she saw a knife in Miss Mason. Think it killed her right off instantly?"

Doc Blane shook his head.

"Singer," he said, "I don't think the knife killed her at all."

"Then what—" I spluttered.

The Doc interrupted me. "But as I say, I have no experience in these things. There will have to be an autopsy. The county medical man is coming this afternoon. He'll make sure."

"The District Attorney seems to think the knife did it," Singer said.

Doc grinned again.

"The District Attorney," he said, "wants to get home. He's afraid he might have to spend the night in Preston. The idea horrifies him."

He got up and slapped the top of his hat.

"Got to run," he said.

"As owner of the hotel," Singer said, "I think I should witness the autopsy."

He smiled. Doc Blane smiled back. Then he said, "I'll see what can be done." He went out.

I looked at Singer. He was gazing into space.

"Yes, sir," Singer said, "gossip is a valuable thing. We know a lot from gossip that we'd have to ask a lot of questions to find out any other way. For instance, everybody knows that Jonathan Rowe, Tommy's father—who, besides owning the First National Bank, is president of the School Board—tried to break up the friendship between Tommy and Marian Mason, and even hauled her before a special meeting of the School Board to reprimand her. But Tommy is a good-for-nothing, as everybody also knows, and the Board couldn't find anything against Marian Mason as a teacher, so that came to nothing. In December, Bill Fogarty joined the army and along in March got into Officer Candidates' School. Everybody was happy about Bill Fogarty, and thought that Marian Mason would have done well to stick to Bill instead of kiting around with Tommy Rowe. But Marian Mason continued to kite around with Tommy Rowe anyway, and some of the gossip got pretty thick."

"Getting kind of dirty, isn't it?" I said.

Singer shrugged.

"'But that was in another country,'" he quoted, "'and besides, the wench is dead.'"

"What now?" I said. "If the District Attorney is in a hurry to get home, it looks like either he will give up or somebody will get railroaded."

"I don't think he'll give up," Singer said.

"Then the salesman from Detroit will get railroaded," I said.

"Maybe," said Singer.

"Maybe he did it after all," I said.

"Maybe."

I got the idea Singer didn't want to talk about the salesman.

"There must be more to the history of Marian Mason than we've mentioned so far."

"There must be a lot more," Singer said.

"How do we find it out?"

"Let's go talk to Mrs. Fogarty," Singer said.

But then the door opened again and somebody came in. It was Curly Evans. And right behind him came Mr. Rowe.

Now this Curly Evans was a big boy. He was over six feet tall and he weighed a solid two hundred and twenty—and I mean solid. They told me that when he played football for Preston High School there were fifteen guys from other teams laid up for most of the season. He was kind of muscle-bound now, but still handy with his fists and not too heavy on his feet. He'd got into professional wrestling for a while a few years back, but it worried his mother so much that he quit and went to work in Ole Davis's machine shop. He was also a plumber and he did odd jobs around town in his spare time. He took good care of his mother until she died, never made any trouble for anybody, kept his mouth shut, and worked hard. Nobody I knew of ever had anything against him. He'd lived in the hotel about a year. He was maybe thirty-two, thirty-three years old and as bald as a billiard ball.

He came in, looked around the room, then, without saying a word, walked over to the love seat and sat down. The thing squeaked and sagged under him and I saw Singer hold his breath till Curly got settled.

Mr. Rowe sat down in a chair near the door. He didn't say anything either. I looked at both of them, then at Singer, and asked, "Who wants a drink?"

They both nodded. I mixed a couple of stiff ones and handed them out. Mr. Rowe sniffed his glass, smiled, and took a swallow. Curly lifted his and drained two-thirds of it in one gulp.

I picked up the phone, rang for Harry Baird and told him to bring in a washtub full of ice and two more quarts of liquor.

Curly grinned, drank the rest of his and set the glass down.

"Can't stay that long, Joe," he said.

Mr. Rowe said: "Curly came to me and said he had a little information somebody might want. I thought we'd tell the county attorney, Weaver, but—"

"Well?" Singer said, looking at Curly.

"I don't like that little squirt, Weaver," Curly said. "They said you was working on this murder case and I figured you'd know what to do—"

He paused, looking for words. Curly wasn't much of a talker.

"Is this information about the murder?" Singer said.

"Well, no," Curly said. "It's about them two kids—Blake's kid and Granger. I got an idea about where they might go."

"We found Blake's kid, you know," I said.

Curly nodded. "Yeah. I know." He looked at us, then down at his hands again. "But the other kid—I don't know. This ain't much—seems kind of silly now I think it over."

"What is it, Curly?" Singer said.

Curly looked at Mr. Rowe.

"Go ahead, Curly," Mr. Rowe said. "Every little bit helps, you know."

"Where do you think young Granger went?" Singer said.

"I think he went to the City," Curly said.

Singer looked at me. I felt a little embarrassed. If that was all Curly knew, it did seem a little silly. I mixed him another drink.

"What makes you think so?" Singer said.

The muscles around Curly's mouth tightened.

"I ain't ready to say that," he said.

"Do you have any idea what part of the City he might have gone to?" Singer asked.

"Yeah," Curly said. "I think you might find him at a certain hotel there."

"Alone?"

Curly shook his head.

"Nope," he said. "With somebody that helped him get out of this hotel last night."

"It might be Don Eastman?" I said.

"It might be," Curly said.

There was a silence. Curly spoke as if he knew what he was talking about. But he was pretty cagy about how he knew it. I didn't know how to take it. I knew Curly spent quite a lot of time around the City and had a lot of connections up there. If he was guessing about what happened to the Granger kid, he must know something else, too. But whatever that was, he wasn't saying.

"Do you think the Granger boy had anything to do with the murder of Miss Mason?" Singer said.

Curly looked at his hands.

"I don't know," he said.

"Were you in your room all night last night?" Singer asked.

"Yeah."

"Did you hear anything unusual?"

"Nope. Slept like a log."

"You didn't hear it when we put those kids to bed at three a.m.?" I said.

He shook his head.

"After all," Mr. Rowe said suddenly, "we're not putting Curly on trial. He merely had some information for you."

He sounded pretty sharp. Singer nodded.

"Of course," he said. "I'm sorry, Curly. And I appreciate your telling us about young Granger."

"That's all right," Curly said, getting up. "I got to get going now. Got to run out to the tourist camp and fix them pipes. Froze again this year."

He went to the door, stopped and looked at Mr. Rowe.

"I can finish that job today," he said. "Anything else to do down there?"

"No, Curly," Mr. Rowe said. "Just the pipes."

"Okay." Curly went out.

Nobody said anything. Mr. Rowe seemed to be embarrassed.

Finally he looked at Singer and said: "I didn't mean to be so short with you. It's just that I feel sort of—responsible for Curly. He's so big and awkward, and he gets confused."

"I understand, Mr. Rowe," Singer said. "I shouldn't have tried to pump him."

There was another silence. Mr. Rowe started to get up, changed his mind, looked around the room, and cleared his throat.

"There's something I ought to tell you," he said. "It's hard for me, but I know you keep things pretty straight in your head. I wouldn't tell Weaver—he'd grab at it and get it all twisted. You're not like Weaver, Singer. You'll walk around a thing and look it over before you make up your mind." He hesitated.

"Yes?" Singer said.

Mr. Rowe cleared his throat again.

"It's this. My boy—Tommy—was in Miss Mason's room last night."

I looked at Singer. Singer's mild blue eyes were gazing at Mr. Rowe, but he didn't have any expression on his face. It surprised me to have Mr. Rowe come out with a thing like that, but you couldn't tell whether it surprised Singer or not. You never can tell what Singer is thinking.

"About what time was that?" Singer said.

"About eleven-thirty," Mr. Rowe said. "I know he was up there because I followed him."

"You followed him?" I said.

Mr. Rowe looked sheepish and nodded his head. "I shouldn't have done it, but I was worried about Tommy's relations with Miss Mason. I—"

He stopped. You could see that he wished he'd never started this at all. Then he said: "But I know he didn't kill her. He couldn't have."

"And how do you know?" Singer said.

"Because I saw him come out of her room. And after he left I could hear her moving around. She was still alive when Tommy left."

I had a professional curiosity about it.

"Just where were you all this time?" I said.

"I was standing just inside the door to the bathroom. I held the door open a crack and I could see the door to Miss Mason's room."

"How long was he with her?" I said.

"About twenty minutes. They were drinking."

"And you were in the bathroom all that time?"

"Yes."

"That was pretty risky, wasn't it? What if Miss Mason happened to—I mean—"

"I would simply have closed the door and locked it."

"Oh," I said.

"Did you follow Tommy out of the hotel," Singer asked, "after he left Miss Mason?"

"Well, no. I was afraid he might stop in the lobby and I didn't want him to see me. I went down the fire escape."

I blinked. "But the fire escape doesn't run past the bathroom," I said. "The bathroom is on the inside—on the court."

"I went through Curly's room. I had to see Curly anyway."

"Curly didn't think it was funny—you going out by way of the fire escape?"

"No. You see, I've had occasion to go to Curly's room several times. He's helped me sometimes—about Tommy, I mean. I've had him watch Tommy, try to keep him out of trouble."

"Curly's the boy that could do it," I said.

And Singer said, "Yes, indeed."

Mr. Rowe got up. He didn't seem to know what to do with his hands.

"I had to tell you this," he said, "about Tommy's being in Miss Mason's room. It was bound to get out sooner or later, and I'd rather have you know the real facts. I don't trust Weaver."

"Thank you," Singer said. "Just one question—"

Mr. Rowe had his hand on the doorknob. "Yes?" he said.

"When Tommy came out of Miss Mason's room last night, was he carrying two drinking glasses?"

Mr. Rowe closed his eyes and thought.

"Now that you mention it," he said, "I believe he was. He had a big paper bag with a bottle of liquor in it. I know that because he had it when he went in, too. And when he came out he had something in the other hand and he was putting it into the bag. I didn't think anything of it at the time, but I guess that's what it was. Glasses. Why? Is it important?"

"I don't know yet," Singer said.

"Well—that's all," Mr. Rowe said. "I know Tommy didn't kill her. I'm sure you'll look at it clearly and find out the truth."

"I hope so," Singer said.

"If there's any way I can help—"

"Thank you, Mr. Rowe," said Singer.

Mr. Rowe went out.

Singer leaned back in his chair and closed his eyes. "Do we go see Mrs. Fogarty now?" I said.

"I guess we do, Joe," Singer said. "I'm afraid it won't be as dramatic as our talk with Curly and Mr. Rowe, but it will have to be done."

"Aren't you going to tell Harley Granger where he can find his kid?"

"Not yet. I want to investigate a little first. I wouldn't want Mr. Granger to be disappointed."

"You think Curly was lying?"

"Oh, no, Joe. Not at all. I'm sure he wasn't lying." I didn't ask any more questions. Singer wasn't in the mood for it.

CHAPTER 6

"Do you suppose Weaver will let me leave the hotel?" I asked.

"Probably," Singer replied. "I think I convinced him of your innocence while you were down cellar, scrapping with the bad-mannered detective."

The uniformed cop was stationed at the main entrance. He looked at me as we went out, but didn't try to stop us.

Mrs. Fogarty lived on a side street a few blocks from the hotel. It took us about six minutes to walk over there. We got there around three-thirty. It was a wide, rambling house, built of white stone, probably a hundred years old, with a porch running all the way across the front and green shutters at the windows. We went around to the back. Mrs. Fogarty was in the kitchen. We went up on the back porch, just walked in through the screen door. The kitchen door was open, and Singer tapped on the wall.

Mrs. Fogarty was one of the sweetest little old ladies in the world. She'd brought Bill up from a baby single-handed, Mr. Fogarty having died a few months after Bill was born. People said he'd been a great guy. A doctor. Mrs. Fogarty had been his nurse and general assistant before they were married. She was older than Mr. Fogarty by several years, and Bill had been born late in her life. She was well along in her sixties now and looked frail. But she was always cheerful, always comforting somebody in trouble.

When Singer tapped on the wall she turned around to see who it was, and her face lighted up and she smiled.

"Well, Singer, and Joe," she said. "Come right in. Excuse me if I just go on with this baking. I'm making a batch of cookies. You know Bill. I told him I'd send him a batch the day after he left. When he was home, y'know, there was so much to talk about I just didn't get around to baking, except from time to time, a pie, or a cake…"

Singer was smiling benevolently.

"Bill will be happy to get these, I'll bet," he said. "What time did he leave last night?"

"Oh, let me see," said Mrs. Fogarty. "He had to get over to Montpelier to catch the train at eleven-thirty. I guess he left here about ten-forty-five. He was driving, you know. He'd borrowed his cousin Jerry's car in Montpelier and he was going to drive back and leave it and then get the train."

"Here," she said, holding out a pan. "You boys always liked my cookies. These are just fresh out of the oven. They're Bill's favorites."

I looked at the cookies. They were small, chocolate cookies filled with bits of nuts. I looked at Singer. He was still smiling.

"Well, thank you ever so much, Mrs. Fogarty," he said. "I hate to rob Bill like this, but it's a cruel world. Every man for himself."

Singer took two or three cookies and Mrs. Fogarty handed them to me. I followed Singer's lead. I ate one. They were certainly good cookies.

Mrs. Fogarty had brought a fresh batch out of the oven. She lifted them off of the cookie sheet and put them on a paper. She washed her hands at the kitchen sink and took off her apron.

"Well," she said, "that's all for now. I won't have to look at those in the oven for fifteen minutes. Won't you come in the parlor and sit down?"

We followed her into the parlor.

Singer sat down in the old Boston rocker. Mrs. Fogarty and I sat on the sofa near the front windows.

"I suppose," Singer said, "you heard about the sad death of Miss Mason."

Mrs. Fogarty made a wry face.

"Well, yes, Singer, I did. It just took my breath away for a minute. Why would anyone take it into his head to do that to such a lovely girl?"

"It's a shame," Singer said. "I understand she'd only lived at the hotel a few days—less than two weeks."

"Yes," said Mrs. Fogarty. "She seemed perfectly happy here up until ten or twelve days ago. She was a good roomer, so neat and clean all the time, and no trouble at all. I was glad to have someone in the house after Bill left and all. Kept me company, even though I didn't really see much of her."

"I don't suppose she had any reason for leaving here," Singer said. "Probably just wanted a little change."

"She didn't give me any reason," Mrs. Fogarty said. "It was just after Bill came home—the day after that party some of the young folks gave Bill, the surprise party."

"Oh?" Singer said.

"She just came in after school and said she was moving to the hotel. I asked her if there was anything wrong and she said, no, nothing at all. She'd just decided that she'd better go over there. She said maybe she'd be out late a few nights and she didn't want to disturb me. I told her it wouldn't disturb me any if she stayed out late, but she said she was afraid it might. She said she'd been very happy here. She was real sweet. I was sorry to see her go."

"There wasn't anything at all that might have made her decide to leave?" Singer said.

Mrs. Fogarty looked at Singer for a while and finally she said, "There was only one thing."

"Yes?" said Singer.

"She had a quarrel with Bill. Oh, it wasn't much, I guess. She went around with Bill for a while, you know, before he went into the army."

"Yes," said Singer, "I remember."

"Well, about a week after Bill had been home on this furlough, it must have been the night before the party, they had a talk. It was late at night. I'd gone to bed. Bill was sitting up, reading, and I heard Miss Mason come in. I was very sleepy and I must have dozed off. The next thing I knew, I was awake and I could hear Bill and Marian talking—pretty loud. I tried not to listen, but I couldn't help hearing some of it."

She stopped. Singer was watching her, smiling all the time, not urging, not sitting on the edge of his seat, but listening. He nodded at Mrs. Fogarty.

"Yes?" he said. "Do you remember what they were saying?"

"Well—" Mrs. Fogarty seemed to be trying hard to remember. "Of course, I don't know what it was all about, but I heard Bill say, 'I wouldn't do that if I were you,' and Marian said, 'I will do it, Bill, whether you think I ought to or not.' Then Bill asked, 'But what proof do you have?' and Marian said, 'I won't need proof.'"

Mrs. Fogarty stopped again.

"You don't know what they were talking about?" said Singer.

"No," said Mrs. Fogarty.

"Did they stop talking after that?"

"Well, they talked some more, but I couldn't make anything out of it. Bill said, 'You'll never make it stick, Marian,' and she said, 'Yes, I will. You've been home a week, haven't you? That's long enough.' And about that time I fell asleep again."

"Did they seem to be really quarreling?" asked Singer.

"Well—yes, they did," said Mrs. Fogarty. "It bothered me for a while. I didn't like to have Bill upset like that when he was home for a rest—these are such trying times for everybody—but he did sound upset. But the next day he didn't mention it and I didn't bring it up. Far as I know, he didn't see Marian after that, except when she came in or went out. Then a few days later she came to me and said she was going to move. I do hope it wasn't anything Bill said to her that made her want to go. I've never had anything against Marian."

"Of course not," Singer said. "I understand you sent her some cookies after she went to the hotel."

"Matter of fact, I did," Mrs. Fogarty said.

"Well, I guess we'd better be running along," Singer said. "Those are awfully good cookies, Mrs. Fogarty, Bill's going to like those."

We got up.

"That reminds me," she said. "I'd better look at the ones that are in the oven now. It was nice of you boys to drop in. I hope you'll come again. I'm so used to having boys around, it seems strange, with Bill gone…"

"We'll drop in again," said Singer. "You take care of yourself now."

"Oh, yes, I haven't much else to do," Mrs. Fogarty said and smiled.

We left by the front door. Mrs. Fogarty stood for a few seconds looking after us before she closed the door to go back into the house.

"Look, Singer," I said, when we were out on the sidewalk again, "I'm getting scared."

"Why?"

"Well—seems to me we're finding things out that we'd just as well not know. Seems to me all the people we think of as the nicest people in town are turning out wrong."

"That's a hasty opinion," Singer said. "If life is a series of unpleasant truths, it is also a series of compensations for them."

"You don't say," I said.

"Never be afraid of the truth, Joe."

"Who's afraid?" I said. "I just want to have a little faith left."

Singer sighed and didn't say anything more and in a little while I began to feel foolish.

"Okay," I said. "So Marian Mason and Bill Fogarty had a fight. What about?"

"That we will have to ferret out," said Singer. "It would occur to Mrs. Fogarty's naive nature to play it down. Maternal solicitude, the protective instinct. I think it must have been a more strenuous quarrel than she made out."

"How do you ferret it out? One party's dead and the other is a hundred miles away in camp."

"I'm going to ask Bill Fogarty."

"You going up to Camp Custer?"

"No, Joe. I'm going to send Bill a telegram."

"That's fine," I said. "He'll send the whole story right back. He's got nothing else to do."

"We'll see, Joe. We'll see."

We were headed back now toward the hotel. Life in Preston had swung to normal after the first buzz of excitement. Groups of people were gathered here and there, and probably they were talking about the murder, but they would have been gathered in the same way any other time, talking about something else. There was no crowd around the hotel.

As we passed the bank we saw Doc Blane come running down the hotel steps and start up the street in our direction. He stopped when he saw Singer.

"I'm on my way to Fisk's funeral parlor," he said. "If you want to witness that autopsy—"

"I'll be right along," Singer said.

Doc looked at me. "But I'm afraid Joe here—" he said.

"Don't apologize, Doc," I said. "I once saw an autopsy. That's once too often."

"What bothered you, Joe?" asked Doc.

"The smell," I said. "I didn't mind anything else. Just the smell."

Doc laughed.

"I've got to get along, Singer," he said.

"Joe," Singer said, "you send a telegram to Bill Fogarty. Inform him of the death of Marian Mason and ask him why they quarreled."

"That all?" I said.

"That's all."

"Okay."

He hurried off to catch up with Doc Blane.

I went down to the D. T. & I. station to send the wire. It read:

> Marian Mason murdered last night. What did you quarrel with her about when you were home? Please reply collect. Singer Batts

I asked old Ezra Cummings, the station agent, to call me at the hotel when he got a reply, and he said he would.

I went back to the hotel and into the sitting room and started in again on the bourbon.

Forty-five minutes later Singer came in. I was itching to know what he had found out, but I was damned if I'd ask. Finally he opened up.

"We know more now, Joe," he said.

"Yeah?"

"Marian Mason died of strychnine poisoning around twelve o'clock last night."

"Yeah?" I said.

"Yes, Joe."

"Then the knife didn't kill her?"

"No."

"You don't say," I said.

"Something else," Singer said.

"What?"

"At the time of her death, Marian Mason was pregnant."

The telephone rang. It was Ezra Cummings. "Got a reply to that wire, Joe," he told me.

"Shoot," I said.

I wrote it down as he read it to me:

Sorry about Marian. As to why we quarreled, ask Curly Evans.

CHAPTER 7

"Curly Evans seems to be the big mind in this business," I said.

Singer didn't hear me. He was gazing at the door. You could practically hear the wheels in his head whirling around, faster and faster. Suddenly he stuck out his jaw—that always meant he'd clicked on an idea—and made for the door.

"Hey," I said, "let's have another shot before we go out."

"No time now, Joe."

So I followed him right away.

I followed him outside and through the kitchen to the back of the hotel into the alley, where the hotel and the stores in that section dumped their trash into big packing cases. The cases were hauled away every two or three days. They were about half full now, which meant they would be hauled away some time tomorrow—maybe.

Singer picked up a long stick and began to poke around in the cases. I watched him. He did it for quite a while. Every now and then he would reach into the rubbish and pull something out. But he always threw it back again and went on poking. Finally he quit and dropped the stick.

"Today's hotel rubbish been dumped?" he asked me.

"Yeah," I said. "About noon. It's four o'clock now. What are we looking for?"

"You work on it for a while, Joe," he said and went on down the alley to the back of the harness shop next door. There was a big box of rubbish there, too, half full, and a smaller one up on the edge of the big box, I started to let this one spill out. Singer grabbed my arm.

"Don't be in a hurry, Joe," he said. "Ease it down. Let the trash trickle out slowly."

So I did that, and Singer got down close to the edge of the big box and watched the trash that rolled into the box: paper, old razor blades, a pair of discarded socks, a pocket mystery book, all kinds of odds and ends.

Every once in a while Singer would stop me and grab something that had started to roll out. But everything he picked up he threw back in.

"What the hell?" I said. "Even if you find something, you don't know where it came from."

He didn't answer that one at all.

My arms were getting pretty tired by this time and I guess I hurried it up too much. The next thing I knew, Singer was hanging over the edge of the packing case, about to split his pants, paddling around in the rubbish, trying to keep up with me. The little box was empty. I dropped it on the ground and started to laugh. Singer pushed himself up out of the case, straightened his coat, and brushed off his pants. His hands were empty. He looked very hurt.

"Well?" I said.

"Nothing," he said, and turned away.

The next place was Benson's Laundry. Benson's rubbish box wasn't in the alley. It was down by the side door between the laundry and the harness shop. They only had one small box and there wasn't much in it. Singer bent over and rummaged around in the trash.

"Now look," I said. "If you're going to go prowling around in other people's rubbish, you can count me out—"

But Singer said, "Ahh!" and came up out of the trash box with something wrapped in newspaper.

"You found it?" I said.

"I think so," he said.

He laid the package on the ground and opened it. There were two drinking glasses.

"That's fine," Singer whispered. "Neither one is broken."

He smelled them, handling them carefully. Then he shook his head and wrapped them up in the newspaper. He put them under his arm and went back to the alley. When he got to the building where Doc Blane's office was, he turned down beside it and went to the street. We went into the Doc's office.

Doc looked at us and made a face.

"The two detectives," he said. "What is it this time?"

Singer took the glasses out of the paper and handed them to the Doc.

"Would you be able to tell whether either or both of these showed any traces of strychnine?" Singer asked.

Doc Blane jumped a little. "Yes," he said, "I could."

"Do you have time?" Singer asked.

"I guess so."

He took the glasses and smelled them, just as Singer had done back in the alley.

"Smells like it," he said, "but I'd better make sure. Just a few minutes."

He went inside and we waited.

He was back in about five minutes with the glasses.

"Where did you find these, Singer?" he asked.

"Out in the alley," said Singer.

"They ought to be turned over to the District Attorney. They probably carry fingerprints."

"By all means," Singer said. "I'll do that, of course. Did you find any strychnine?"

Slowly the Doc nodded. "Yes, I did."

"In both?"

"No. Only one."

"Which one?"

"That one. I stuck a piece of tape on it."

"I see," said Singer.

We got up. The Doc followed us to the door. He was very serious.

"Singer," he said, "do you think you know who killed Miss Mason?"

Singer laughed. "No, Doctor, I don't," he said. "Not yet."

The Doc thought it over. Then he shrugged.

"You'd better turn those glasses over to the District Attorney," he said.

"Certainly," Singer said.

"When you get through with them," said the Doc, and went back into his office.

"Back to the hotel?" I said to Singer.

"Not yet, Joe," he said.

"You going to turn those glasses over to Weaver?"

"Yes, sooner or later."

I looked at Singer. "What next?"

"Where's your car, Joe?"

"Back of the bank."

"You have gasoline?"

"Are you kidding?"

"Could we drive, say, five miles?"

"All right. We'll take a chance. Where are we going?"

"We're going down to the tourist camp to see Curly Evans."

"We can't wait till he gets back to the hotel?"

"We can't wait, Joe."

"All right."

We went to the car and I got it started.

* * * *

The tourist camp was not much more than a glorified swimming hole, a mile north of town. Nobody had ever been known to camp there. But it made a nice little recreation spot. They'd dammed up the creek and, while it wasn't any swank resort, you could swim in it. And they'd built a bath-house, with showers, where people could put on their bathing suits. Every year the pipes that fed the showers froze and some of them burst. They also had to plug up the holes the boys drilled between their side of the bathhouse and the girls' side. They paid Curly Evans a dollar an hour to take care of these things every spring. He was pretty late this year, but we'd had a cold spring and nobody had wanted to go swimming yet.

"What do you think Curly knows about the murder?" I said.

"I don't know that he knows anything about the murder, Joe, but apparently he knows something about the quarrel that Bill Fogarty had with Miss Mason."

"Maybe that quarrel doesn't have anything to do with the murder."

"That is possible."

"You wouldn't say offhand that Bill Fogarty had killed her, would you?"

"I wouldn't say that offhand about anybody, Joe."

And that was all I could get out of Singer during the ride.

I shuddered when I turned into the side road leading into the camp. My tires were like paper now and that road was a washboard made of jagged rocks. Singer sat on his side clutching the handle of the door. I swerved once to miss a big one and he bumped his head against the window. It seemed to wake him up.

"Almost there?" he muttered.

"Yeah. It was a tough fight, Ma."

We dipped down and wound toward the camp. There were trees and thick bushes that hung over each side of the road and swished against the sides of the car as we passed. Then we got into the woods where the road twisted among tall old trees that cut out most of the sunlight. It was always gloomy in that patch of woods.

Hell of a place to build a camp, I thought.

We wound around some more and finally came into the little clearing where the building stood. Curly Evans's old Ford was parked a little off the road and I pulled up behind it. There was nobody in sight and we couldn't hear anybody working.

"Must be having himself a smoke," I said.

We got out of the car and started toward the bathhouse. All the doors on the near side were open and you could see at a glance that Curly was not in any of the rooms. We went around the corner to the other side. All those doors were open, too, except one—at the far end. Curly was not in any of the open rooms.

We tried the door of the last room. It wouldn't open. It wasn't exactly locked, but there was something in the way, something heavy, that gave a little. I was about to let go at the door with my shoulder when Singer stopped me.

"Go into the next booth," he said, "and look over."

The partitions between the rooms were not built up to the ceiling. You could take hold at the top, pull yourself up and look over into the next room.

I went into the second room from the end. Singer followed me. I got a good grip on the top of the partition and hoisted myself. I locked my elbows and took a breath. Then I looked over into the next room.

At first I almost lost my hold. I must have made a noise of some kind because I heard Singer ask, "What is it, Joe?"

"It's Curly," I said.

He was huddled over on the floor, his head jammed against the door, and there was blood all over his back, soaking through his denim shirt.

I told Singer.

"Is he dead?" Singer asked.

"I don't know." I called, "Curly!"

I don't know whether it was because I called or not, but pretty soon he moved—moved his head away from the door and lifted up from his waist a little.

"Curly," I said again, and this time his hands moved.

"Tell him to crawl away from the door," Singer said.

"Curly," I said once more, "can you hear me?"

He lifted his head slightly, then dropped it forward.

"Try to crawl back from the door some," I said, "so we can get to you."

I repeated it three times. Then at last, slowly, inch by inch, he rolled to one side and got on to his hands and knees. It broke my heart to watch him, the big bruiser, crawling like a baby, his head sagging and that blood on him. It was like watching a sick dog or horse.

"Look, Singer," I said. "I'll let myself down the other side and help Curly out of the way. You open the door from outside."

I skinned up to the top of the partition and swung over. It was tough going down. I had to push out and away from the wall to keep from stepping on Curly. I almost tore my arms loose, but I made it without landing on him.

I knelt down and got one of Curly's arms around my shoulders. I held onto his arm and put mine under his back. It was sticky under there. I didn't like getting that blood all over me.

He opened his eyes when I moved him and looked at me. But he didn't seem to be able to tell who it was. He muttered something, but I couldn't make it out. Singer was opening the door from outside and I pulled Curly clear. Singer helped me get a grip on him and we started to ease him out onto the grass. Those little dressing cubicles weren't big enough for anybody to stretch out in.

"Take it easy now," Singer said. "Maybe he has a chance."

"He don't look like it," I said.

"Lot of blood."

"Yeah. All over me."

"It will wash off," Singer said.

We got Curly out on the grass beside the bathhouse and rolled him over. Singer took out a pocket knife and cut away part of Curly's shirt. It was soaked with blood and in one spot under his left shoulder blade it was stuck to him. There was a little hole in the shirt at that point and that was where the blood had come from.

"Shot," Singer said.

"You don't say," I said.

"Get that first-aid kit out of your car, Joe."

I ran to the car for the kit. When I got back to Singer he had cut away more of the shirt and was crouched down close to Curly's head, talking to him. I handed him the kit.

"He's trying to say something," Singer said.

"He tried in there, too. I couldn't make it out."

Singer took a sterile dressing out of the kit and laid it over the little hole in Curly's back. Then he rolled him onto his back and lifted his head a little and held it. Curly's lips were moving, but no sound came out.

"Hey," I said. "Shouldn't we tell somebody about this?"

"Indeed," Singer said. "Suppose you run up to Seton's place and call Doctor Blane."

"I better call the District Attorney, too," I said.

Singer frowned, shook his head.

"No. Just call Doctor Blane. In the meantime, I will try to understand what Curly is trying to say."

"Good luck," I said and went off, across the field back of the tourist camp toward the Seton's place up on the highway.

* * * *

When I got back to the bathhouse, Singer was washing Curly's face with some muddy water that he had probably got out of the creek.

"Doc's coming right out," I said.

"And Mr. Weaver?" Singer asked.

"No. I talked him out of that. He said the only person he really had to tell was Pete Haley. He's going to tell Pete and bring him out if he wants to come."

"Good," Singer said.

"Did Curly talk?"

"Since you left he's said just three words. He's out of his head and he doesn't say who shot him. Just three words."

"What three words?"

"He says, 'Hotel Sheraton—City.' Just like that, over and over. Three words. 'Hotel Sheraton—City'!"

"Never heard of it," I said. "Maybe he's got a girl there, or something."

"Or it might be the place where the Granger boy is hiding," Singer said. "I don't know how much longer Curly's got."

"He's out of his head," I said. "He might say anything."

"I know. But he says it as though he were trying to make me understand it."

About then Curly opened his eyes and looked up at us. His eyes were clearer than I had seen them since we found him. He looked straight at Singer and his lips moved a little, and then I could hear him saying, very softly, "Go to Sheraton Hotel—City."

That seemed to be all he could manage at one time. His eyes closed again and his head fell back and lolled over to one side.

We heard a car coming down the road into the camp.

"That would be Doc Blane," I said.

Singer was bending low over Curly.

"Listen, Curly," he said. "Who shot you? Tell us who shot you?"

Curly's eyes opened again and he looked first at Singer and then at me, but he didn't answer.

"Maybe he don't know who shot him," I said. "After all, he got it in the back. Some dirty bastard—"

"I just thought he might be able to guess," Singer said.

The car we had heard came rolling into sight and pulled up behind my jalopy. The Doc and Pete Haley got out and came toward us. Doc was carrying his bag. Pete already had his hat off and was mopping his face, looking worried.

Doc said nothing, but squatted down beside Curly and went to work. Pete began to make funny little growling noises.

"What next!" he said. "What next! Murders and killin's and people gittin' shot—"

"That covers everything," I said.

"Who done it, Singer?" Pete asked.

Singer shook his head. "I wish I knew, Pete," he said.

Doc Blane got up. I had been listening to Pete and hadn't paid any attention to Curly.

"He's dead," Doc said. "He never had a chance."

I'll never be able to explain this, but when the Doc said that and I looked down and saw that big hunk of guy and knew he would never get up again, a big lump came in my throat. I had never been a special friend of Curly's, but I had known him the way you know people in a little town, and had heard stories about him that were more like legends than anything else, and I had come to have a great respect for him. It didn't seem right.

Curly had been a simple kind of guy, no angel. He had batted around plenty—both liquor and women—and he was a tough egg in a combat. But he had never been known to hurt anybody who didn't deserve to be hurt. He had helped a lot of people in our town, one way and another, without making any fuss about it. He had been tough and hard, but he had always been on hand when something good had to be fought for and he had always been on the right side. And now somebody who had not been on the right side had sneaked up behind him and knocked him off.

I began to get a little sore.

"I hope you find the rat that did this," I said, "and I hope I'm around when you do."

"You know, Joe," Singer said, "I was thinking the same thing."

Doc Blane cleared his throat.

"Pete," he said, "you stay here with Curly. I'll go back to town and send the hearse to pick him up."

"We'll go back to town, too," Singer said.

Pete mopped his face. It was clear he didn't want to be left alone with the body, but he was ashamed to say so.

"All right," he said. "Hurry it up."

We followed Doc to his car, where he turned to Singer.

"You have any ideas about this one?" he asked.

"Yes," Singer said.

"You want to come in with me and talk to Mr. Weaver?"

"No," Singer said. "I'm not ready to talk to Mr. Weaver yet. Joe and I have a little trip to make first. Has Mr. Weaver got hold of that traveling salesman yet?"

"Yes," Doc said. "I think Weaver will be leaving soon."

"He's going to charge that man with murder?"

"That's the way it looks."

"Mr. Weaver still thinks he did it?"

"Yes."

"With a knife?"

"No. We convinced him that she was poisoned. He revised his theory. He thinks the salesman got into her room and got acquainted—for no good purpose, you may be sure—and they had a couple of drinks, and when the salesman tried to get fresh and she didn't come across, he tried to knock her out by doping her drink. Then he found he'd given her too much, so he went back to his room, got one of his knives and stuck it in her, in order to throw the police off the track."

"That sounds stupid even to me," I said.

"Very interesting," Singer said. "It has the advantage of simplicity and directness. The attorney doesn't have to clutter his mind up with a number of suspects."

"Has anybody told him," I asked, "that Tommy Rowe went up to Miss Mason's room last night with a package containing liquor, ice, and so on?"

Doc started. "Tommy Rowe? Why, no. I'm sure he hasn't heard about that."

"That would be a good thing to tell Mr. Weaver," Singer said.

Doc studied Singer for a minute and then got into his car. He started up, then stopped and stuck his head out of the window. "You don't think it was Tommy Rowe, do you, Singer?"

"I don't know, Doctor."

Doc drove off.

Singer looked impatient.

"We'll have to go back to the hotel," he said.

"That's all right," I said. "I've got blood all over me. I can change into my last suit."

We climbed into the car and headed back to town. Singer was keeping his mouth shut tight.

CHAPTER 8

It was five-thirty when we went into the hotel through the back door.

"You want me right away?" I said.

"No," Singer said. "I want to talk to Weaver."

"Then I'll change my clothes."

"All right, Joe."

Singer went on to the lobby and I slipped into the suite. I didn't bother to pull the door to. In a little place like Preston people are pretty careless about locking doors. You get in the habit of trusting everybody.

I went into my room and hauled down my last clean suit—I've got three altogether. It was a plaid job that I saved for special occasions, like the stag banquet the Eagles threw every spring up at the Lake. I figured it was a sort of symbol of my progress. All I had when I met Singer and went to work for him was a pair of corduroys, a blue denim shirt, and a bundle of rags. Now I was no longer a bum. I was a businessman, with three suits. In Preston that was high. Most guys had two—one to work in and one to dress up in. I never figured it out. I wasn't so careful with my money.

I was zipping up my pants when I heard the door to the suite squeak and somebody pussyfooting into the living room. I strolled out there.

It was Tommy Rowe. He was bending over my desk, looking for something. I noticed when he touched a paper that it shook like a leaf in a gale.

"Hello, Tommy."

He jerked away from the desk as if he'd heard a shot. He looked at me and then half-grinned.

"Lose something?" I said.

"That envelope, Joe, that I gave you this morning. Since Marian's dead—"

"Oh—sure. I should have given you that before. Been busy."

I pulled open the middle drawer of the desk, hauled the envelope out, and handed it to him.

He looked at it, turned it over, spotted the loose flap.

"I sealed it," he said.

"Yeah?" I shrugged.

He was only whispering when he said, "Who opened it, Joe?"

I felt like a worm, but I had to keep clear on this little deal.

"I didn't," I said, "and Singer didn't. I've got no idea what's in it."

"You think it was Weaver?"

"Don't see how. It's been in here all the time. I never did put it in her box."

"Maybe"—he brightened up a little—"I only thought I sealed it."

"Maybe."

"Well, thanks, Joe," he said, and started to leave.

Then he stopped. He had something else on his mind. But he wasn't getting it out very fast. I tried to help him along.

"Curly Evans got knocked off this afternoon," I said.

"He did?"

His eyes stared through me. He closed them, then opened them wide. "You think it was the same person that killed Marian?"

"I don't know. Curly had a couple of angles on her murder."

"It's too bad. Curly was a good fellow."

"The best."

Tommy stood there for a minute and then started away again.

"What's on your mind, Tommy?" I asked.

He stopped. I had a hunch he was glad I'd asked him. Gave him a start.

"Well...there's something... I guess I ought to tell somebody, even though it looks bad for me. But I didn't kill her. Really."

"Okay," I said.

"It's only—Last night I went up to Marian's room."

"When?"

"About eleven o'clock. I took a bottle of whisky and some ice up with me and we had a few drinks. I did that every once in a while."

"Some hotel I'm managing," I said. "Wonder we don't get run out of town... Go ahead."

"The important thing is that somebody else was up there—"

"With Miss Mason?"

"No. I mean on the same floor—watching."

"Watching what?"

"I'm not sure. But whoever it was, he watched me come out of her room. He was in the bathroom, and I noticed when I left her room that the bathroom door was partly open, and suddenly somebody pushed it shut— or almost—just as I stepped out into the hall."

"That could have been an accident, a coincidence."

"I don't think so," Tommy said. "He didn't slam the door shut the way you would if you were just going in there and didn't give a damn. He pushed it to fast, but he didn't let it click. He kept it quiet."

"You've got no idea who it was?"

"No."

"Might have been a woman."

"It might have been."

Because of those bare footprints on the window-sill in Marian Mason's room, I kept coming back to the theory that a woman had come into the room from the fire escape and killed her. I hadn't discussed it with Singer yet and I couldn't figure out what woman in Preston would have killed her. But it nagged at my mind.

"You left Marian alive?" I said.

"Yes."

"It's none of my business," I said, "but why did you go up to see her? Just a social visit?"

"Well—" He hesitated. "I wanted to talk with her."

"About her being pregnant?"

He was startled. "You know about that?" he said.

"Yeah. Autopsy brought it out."

He shuddered. "I wanted to marry her," he said. "I would have. I was going to, anyway…"

"Anyway what?"

"In spite of what my father told me."

I waited.

"He told me that if I married her, he'd disown me—make me leave the bank—even leave town. I couldn't face that. I—to tell you the truth, Joe, I don't think I could hold a job anywhere else. I'm—all shot to pieces. Father knows that."

"What did he have against Marian?"

"I don't know, really. He wouldn't tell me. He was vague about it. I think he knew something about her that nobody else knew. He hated her. He tried to have her fired, you know. But teachers are hard to get now, and she was a good teacher."

"Could it have been your fault she was going to have a kid?"

He blushed a little. "It could," he said. "I don't think it was."

"Who else could it have been?"

"I don't know. She wasn't with me all the time. She'd run off by herself a lot. She said she went to the City, or over to Montpelier—to visit friends. I only saw her once or twice a week."

"She wanted you to marry her—after she found she was pregnant?"

"Yes. She even threatened me. Said she'd go to my father."

"Did she?"

"Yes. She went out to the house one night. I wasn't home. I came in just as she was leaving."

"You didn't talk to her then?"

"Not with Father there. I didn't dare."

"When was this?"

"About four days ago."

I noticed he was getting the shakes in earnest now. "You better go get a drink," I said. "You're in bad shape."

"I know, Joe. I just wanted to let Singer know about last night. Maybe whoever was watching me was the one who killed her. I was afraid to tell Weaver."

"Sure," I said. "I'll tell Singer."

"All right." He went out, closing the door behind him.

I went back to my room and finished dressing.

So Tommy Rowe knew that somebody had been watching him when he went up to Marian's room. But evidently he didn't know who it was.

I got my coat on, put on my hat, and started through the living room toward the lobby. But before I could get there, the door opened and Singer came in, followed by Weaver, both of his dicks, and a stranger who looked pretty fed up.

Singer was getting sore. I could tell by the way he left everybody standing around, marched over to the table, and poured himself a drink.

"Having a party?" I said.

Weaver just snorted, meaning he was sore, too. But I didn't care about that.

"Sit down," Singer said vaguely.

The stranger, looking bored and disgusted, sat down in the easy chair and put his hands in his lap. I saw that they'd handcuffed him. I gave him a cigarette and lit it for him.

"Thanks," he said.

"Joe," Singer said, "this is Mr. Pfeffer, who was a guest of ours last night and whom Mr. Weaver suspects of having murdered Miss Mason. Perhaps Mr. Weaver will be good enough to explain his suspicions."

Singer sat down in his rocker and looked out the window.

"It's simple," Weaver said. "This guy had a sample case full of knives exactly like the one that killed the victim. The victim was a beautiful girl. This guy sneaked into her room and got fresh. When she wouldn't come across—after a few drinks—he got sore and let her have it."

"Fine," I said, "only she was poisoned."

"He did that first," Weaver said. "Poisoned her drink. Then later he was afraid it might not have killed her, so he sneaked in again and stuck the knife in her."

I guess my mouth was hanging open. The guy—Pfeffer—took a long drag on his cigarette and said softly, "My God!"

"It's quite a theory," I said. "But we happen to know that somebody else went up to Miss Mason's room to have a few drinks. And when he left, he took the liquor with him."

"Who?" Weaver said.

I looked at Singer. He nodded his head slightly.

"Kid name of Tommy Rowe," I said.

"The banker's son?"

"Yes, but he didn't kill her."

"What makes you so sure?" Weaver said.

"Because he said so."

Weaver snorted again.

"I have a few questions I'd like to ask Mr. Pfeffer," Singer said.

Weaver was getting confused and curious. He didn't like having Singer butt in, but he wanted to find out what he was thinking. "All right," he said, "but hurry it up."

"Do you mind?" Singer said to Pfeffer.

"Go ahead," Pfeffer said. "I might as well talk to you as anybody."

"First," Singer said, "I'd like to know how many people you heard or saw out on the fire escape the night of the murder."

"What the hell!" Mr. Weaver exclaimed.

Pfeffer's eyes narrowed a little and he looked at Singer with a little interest.

"I didn't *see* any," he said. "I *heard* four."

"That is," Singer said, "you heard somebody out on the fire escape four different times."

"That's right."

"But you couldn't say whether they were four different people or only one or two different people several times."

"There were at least two."

"How do you make that out?"

"They walked different. One was a woman. I heard her voice."

"You heard all that stuff going on outside your window," Mr. Weaver said, "and didn't even get up to look?"

"Hell," said the guy, "I was tired. All I wanted was to go to sleep. I figured it was some guy sneaking in to see his girl. I didn't pay any attention."

"Not till later," Weaver said, "when you went in and tried to make the dame and she wouldn't come across. So you poisoned her and stabbed her."

"Oh, sure," the salesman said. "Then I hanged her with an invisible rope. I also shot her, but it was such a small bullet you couldn't see the hole. I would have strangled her, too, only I was tired out by that time."

I laughed. Weaver looked at me. "What's so funny to you, little man?" he said.

"The whole goddam county government," I said.

The salesman started singing *Stars and Stripes Forever.* "Shut up," Weaver said.

Singer said: "One other question. You sold some knives here, didn't you?"

"Yeah. I took some orders."

"To whom did you sell?"

"I got a big order from the hardware people, and I sold a couple of grocery stores and the bakery."

"The bakery," Singer said. "Did you merely take the order, or did you have the products on hand?"

"I had 'em. They only wanted two—a big one and a small one. I had 'em with me."

"Have you seen the knife they found in the murder victim?"

"Yeah. It was one of mine."

"Was it like the large one you sold to the bakery?"

"Exactly," the guy said.

"That's all," Singer said. Then to Weaver, "Why don't you take the handcuffs off this man so he can smoke easily?"

"He's a suspect," Weaver said. "I'm going to turn him in tonight—or this morning, if you ever get through fooling around."

"You really think he did it?" Singer said.

"Sure," said Weaver, but he didn't look sure. "Anyway, what's all this about selling a knife to the bakery?"

Singer's voice was as patient as ever, but anybody who knew him could feel the edge on it a mile away.

"The bakery employs a chap named Don Eastman," he said. "He lives in this hotel, only two rooms removed from the scene of the crime. He is known to have been intimately associated with the victim. Lastly, he disappeared from the hotel this morning and he has not been seen around town since."

There was a silence. You could tell Weaver was chewing on it.

"And if that's not enough evidence to throw doubt into your case, there is the murder of Curly Evans, of which I have lately informed you. It is unlikely that Mr. Pfeffer, picked up by the police in Detroit some four hours ago, could have killed Curly Evans, who died only forty-five minutes ago."

"I'm not saying he killed Evans."

"And yet," Singer said, "as I have told you, Curly Evans had given us some information which may have an important bearing on the crime."

There was another silence.

"Mr. Weaver," Singer went on, "if you will give me until midnight tonight, I will prove to you absolutely that Mr. Pfeffer could not possibly have committed this crime. I will also prove who did. And I will turn the real murderer over to you."

"You sound pretty sure of yourself," Weaver said. "You know now who the murderer really is?"

"I believe I do," Singer said. "But I can't prove it. I need some time to make sure."

"Why don't you just tell me what you know and let me follow it through? I have legal standing. I can make arrests."

"You, operating as an officer of the law, couldn't possibly get the information we need to complete the case."

"Why don't you let me be the judge of that?"

"It wouldn't do any good," Singer said. "If I told you what I think you wouldn't believe it. If you went ahead and acted on it, you wouldn't be able to get anywhere." Weaver thought it over.

"All I need is six hours," Singer said. "At midnight I'll have the answer. If I'm not back by midnight, you can leave right away."

"I can leave any time I'm ready," Weaver said, "whether you're back or not. Anyway, where are you going? The murder happened here. Why do you have to take a trip?"

"A part of the answer to this problem lies in the City. That's in another state. You have no jurisdiction," Singer said. He looked at his watch. "I have no more time to argue. For my own satisfaction, I am going to follow the case through. You do as you like. Joe and I must be on our way."

He started for the door.

"Wait a minute," Weaver said. "Don't be nasty about it. I'll give you until midnight. But your friend Spinder"—he jerked his thumb at me—"he stays here."

Singer looked at him out of his big blue eyes.

"That's ridiculous," he said.

"No, it isn't. I'm holding him as a material witness. I'm still not satisfied about that marriage license I found with his name on it."

"What the hell!" I said.

"You've done some suspicious moving around here today, Spinder. I'm not taking any chances. I think you know more than you've let on."

"You going to let one of your boys work me over while Singer's gone?" I said.

That burned him. "Enough of that," he said. "I'm just holding you."

"As a hostage, no doubt," Singer said.

I don't think I've ever seen Singer so sore as he was then.

I looked hard at Singer, trying to tell him to go ahead, that they wouldn't hold me for long. I don't know whether he got it or not, but after a minute he said: "Very well. Suit yourself. If you're here at midnight, I'll have the murderer for you."

He went out.

I went over to my desk and poured a drink. The salesman named Pfeffer watched me. He sat very still in his chair, the smoke from his cigarette curling up around his face. Weaver stood in the middle of the room, looking sillier than usual. His two dicks shifted from one foot to the other, looking first at Weaver, then at me, then at Pfeffer.

I heard the six-o'clock bus draw up opposite the hotel and imagined Singer climbing on. I wanted to catch that bus, and I knew how I could do it, but I'd have to get started pretty soon.

I poured a drink for Pfeffer and took it to him. He said, "Thanks," and handed me what was left of his cigarette. I snuffed it out in an ash tray on my desk and picked up my own glass.

"Well, Mr. Holmes," I said to Weaver, "what's the play? Shall I turn on the radio? Shall we dance?"

Weaver snorted. He was the best snorter I had ever heard.

He was saved from making some stupid remark by a knock on the door. Weaver opened it himself. It was Doc Blane.

"I've a report on the death of Curly Evans," Doc said, "if you care to hear it."

It was plain that Weaver wanted to get away. He jerked his head at the dick in plain clothes. To the uniform he said: "You watch these two birds, Connally. If either one tries to make a break, let 'em have it."

I laughed. Weaver threw me a terrible look and stamped out, followed by the other dick, who slammed the door behind him.

I sat down by the desk and took a couple of swallows. The cop sat down on the love seat near the window.

We were lined up diagonally across the room. The dick on the love seat, then Pfeffer in the easy chair, out from Singer's table, then me—at my desk. I caught Pfeffer's eye and tried to stare a message into him. The City bus had been gone for at least three minutes. The next stop would be eight miles up the line, in Bridgeville. It would take the bus fifteen or twenty minutes. I could make it in ten minutes, if I had enough gas, and I thought I had.

Everything depended on Pfeffer. If he caught on, I could do it. If he didn't I might get six months for clipping an officer of the law. I had to take my chances with Pfeffer.

I took one more swallow, set my glass down—it was half-full—wiped my mouth with the back of my hand and stood up.

Connally the cop stood up with me.

"Where do you think you're going?" he said.

He was pretty nervous. Murder was no doubt out of his line. Self-consciously, he reached around and unsnapped his holster.

I shrugged. "After all," I said, "when a guy has to go—you can't object to that."

"Wait a minute!" Connally said.

He hesitated. I turned and started toward the bathroom door.

"Hey! Wait a minute!" he said.

I kept going, wondering whether he was reaching for that big rod he packed.

"Hey!" he said, and I heard him take heavy steps.

I was at the bathroom door now and I looked back. Connally—jerking at his gun, which seemed to be stuck—was moving after me. Just as he got to the easy chair, Pfeffer stretched both his legs out suddenly and caught Connally just below the knees. Connally, his eyes on me, crumpled and sprawled all over the floor, cursing. His gun fell out of the holster. I heard Pfeffer say, "Sorry," and saw him start to get up. Then I was in the bathroom with the door shut and locked behind me.

I went on into my bedroom and opened the door into the kitchen. We'd had a door cut in there so Dora could get into the suite with our meals without having to go through the lobby. It came in handy.

Dora was alone in the kitchen, cooking. I walked fast across the room, saying, "If a cop comes in here, tell him I went down cellar."

As I went through the door and down the back steps, Dora asked, "Will you boys be home for supper? It's 'most ready."

I hit the alley running. My car was sitting behind the bank, headed out toward the street, for once.

It looked like a clear road. Three jumps, into the seat—car still warm, step on the gas and bango! Hi-ho Silver!

How wrong I was.

As I reached the edge of the area-way between the hotel and the bank, somebody stepped out in front of me. I tried to dodge past him and he grabbed my shoulder and spun me around. I looked up. It was Olson, Weaver's big bruiser.

He'd lost his grip when I turned so fast and he was reaching for me now with both hands.

I had a terrible hate for that lug and I wasn't going to let him hold me up now. I hauled back my right leg and threw my foot into his groin with everything I had. He gave a funny little scream and doubled over. I hunched down and hit him with my shoulder. It knocked him over and he rolled away. I stepped wide as he reached for my ankle and beat it across the area-way. I climbed into the car, turned on the ignition, and got her started. As I drove away, I looked back and saw Olson getting to his knees.

The alley went on for two blocks beyond Oak Street and I stayed in it. There was nothing in sight on Oak Street so I didn't even have to stop.

I was hitting fifty in the middle of the next block and I slowed a little as I approached High Street. Nobody coming there, either, so I tore across High and into the last block of the alley. I had to watch myself here, because the alley ran behind houses and people were pretty careless about where they dumped their trash.

So I was going pretty slow when I reached Brick Avenue. And it was a good thing because a girl was walking down the sidewalk, across the alley, and she wasn't looking at me. Even though I was going slow I had to slam the brakes on to keep from hitting her, and my tires screeched on the pavement. That scared the girl. She jumped and looked around. Then she came over to the car. It was Elsie Schaffner.

"Are you going to Bridgeville?" she said.

I jumped. "How did you know?"

"I didn't. I just wondered. Would you give me a lift, please?"

"I shouldn't," I said, "but I will."

She got in and slammed the door, and without wasting any more time I turned into Brick Avenue and headed for Front Street. Front Street was County Highway 17 and led straight into Bridgeville. Once beyond the town limits I could burn up the road. Olson was probably following me, but the county line was only three miles up the road and he couldn't go beyond that. I figured I still had ten minutes. If I could pass the bus on the way I could make it. But I didn't think I could get far beyond Bridgeville. Not enough gas.

"You going to the dance?" Elsie said.

"No," I said, "I'm not going to any dance."

Then I wasn't edgy any more about her asking if I was going to Bridgeville. They had a dance in Bridgeville every Saturday night in the Lions' Hall. A lot of people from Preston went to it every week. I'd forgotten about it. Mostly the fellows went stag and the girls went alone or in packs, and they'd get together at the dance.

I was keeping my mind on the car and the road, not saying anything. Elsie sat over by the door, holding on to the handle. She was a pretty kid, a senior in high school, a nice girl.

After a minute she said, "You seem to be in an awful hurry. Where are you going?"

"I'm trying to catch the City bus," I said.

"Who's on the bus?"

"Singer Batts is on it."

Elsie looked out the window.

"Wasn't it awful about Miss Mason?" she said.

"Yeah. Did you like Miss Mason?"

She looked at me. Then she said, as if she really wanted me to believe it, "Sure I did."

"Was she a good teacher?"

"She was a swell teacher."

I was making sixty-eight now and we were bouncing around a lot. We had to talk pretty loud to make ourselves heard. I rounded a bend in the road and felt better. Far ahead I could see the tail lights of the bus.

"You used to run around with her on double dates, didn't you?" I asked Elsie.

"Once in a while."

"With Don Eastman?"

She hesitated, then said, "I don't go with Don Eastman anymore."

"Why not?"

"Just because," she said.

I pushed the gas clear down. The tail lights of the bus were closer now.

"What was it about Miss Mason that some people didn't like?" I said. "I mean—besides the fact that she smoked and drank and ran around a lot."

There was a long pause this time. Then Elsie said, "I don't know what you're talking about."

"I think you do," I said. And when she didn't answer, I asked, "Seen Don Eastman today?"

"You ask too many questions," Elsie said.

It was at that point I caught up with the bus. I quit talking, sat on the horn, and started around. The driver wouldn't move over. The road wasn't any too wide and I needed all the room I could get. I blinked my lights. He moved over a little. It was just barely enough and there were deep ditches on both sides. But I had to get around him. I blew hell out of my horn, kept flashing my lights, and pushed the accelerator to the floor.

"Be careful, Joe!" Elsie said, grabbing the door handle.

"Take it easy," I said. "It's almost over."

A car was coming toward us and I couldn't tell how far away he was, but it was too late to go back. I just hung on and prayed. I went too far to the left, hit the gravel shoulder, and we swayed. Elsie hollered and closed her eyes. Then I cut in front of the bus and straightened up to let the oncoming car pass. It wasn't wasting any time either.

"My goodness!" Elsie said. "Are you trying to commit suicide?"

Ahead were the lights of Bridgeville, faint in the early evening.

"What about it?" I said to Elsie. "What do you know about Miss Mason that you're not telling?"

"Please, Joe," Elsie said. "No more questions."

"What are you afraid of?" I said. "Eastman?"

"No!" Elsie said. "I'm not afraid of *him*."

"You're afraid of something," I said.

We passed the town limits of Bridgeville and I slowed down a little.

"Maybe I am, Joe," Elsie said. "But I can't tell you about it. I can't tell anybody."

"Not even Singer Batts?"

"No," Elsie said. "I would trust Singer Batts more than anybody else I know. But I couldn't tell this even to him."

"Look," I said. "When somebody commits murder, the law has to find him and take care of him. If you know something about a murder and you don't tell it, you're disobeying the law. If we got no law, we got no safety. Think it over, Elsie."

She didn't say anything.

I pulled up in front of McCarthy's drugstore, where the bus stopped in Bridgeville. I took the car keys out and handed them to Elsie.

"If there's enough gas in the tank," I said, "you can drive this thing home for me after the dance. But go by the back road and leave the car on a side street. The cops will be looking for it."

"All right, Joe," she said. "Thanks for the lift."

"It's okay," I said. "Just think over what I told you."

She walked away. I climbed out of the car just as the bus drew up and honked. The guy who ran the drugstore came out and waved his hands, showing there weren't any passengers. I knocked on the door of the bus and the driver opened it up. I climbed in. The driver looked me over.

"You the guy damn near run me off the road?" he said.

"Sure," I said. "Why didn't you give me room?"

"I ought to turn you in," he said. "You're wild. I got responsibilities. I got passengers."

"Not many, you haven't," I said.

I looked back in the bus. He had one passenger. Singer Batts.

I went back and sat down beside Singer.

He hadn't seen me get on. When I sat down he looked at me.

"Hello, Joe," he said.

"Hi," I said.

The driver shifted gears and we started off.

CHAPTER 9

"I have a couple of minor reports to make," I said to Singer as we rolled out of Bridgeville.

"Good," Singer said.

"First, about Tommy Rowe. I had a little talk with him just before you and Weaver came in with Pfeffer." I told him what Tommy had said. He winced when I came to the lie I told Tommy about opening the envelope. But he didn't say anything, and I couldn't tell whether what Tommy said was interesting to him.

Then I told him about picking up Elsie Schaffner and what she said. That seemed to make a better impression on him than what I told him about Tommy Rowe. When I got through, he said:

"I couldn't do anything without you, Joe. As an observer you are absolutely first-rate. A sort of high-fidelity reporter, you might say. The report of your inspection of the murder room and the events of the morning was amazing. Do you ever miss anything?"

"I miss plenty," I said. "Right now I miss the point of everything that's happened. I have no idea who killed Marian Mason, or how it was done. The evidence makes no sense to me."

"You've been too busy to think about it," Singer said. "You're a man of action. I am so lazy physically that I have plenty of time to interpret the meaning of your actions and observations."

"How about letting me in on it?" I said. "I'd like to know what you think."

"Well, since we have the bus to ourselves and a little time, maybe we ought to review the case. The first thing we have to do is to reconstruct the scene of the crime. We have to know how it happened before we can determine who did it."

"Where do we start?"

"Just to sharpen up our memories, Joe, we'll go over the details of the scene of the murder. What did you find when you went up to Miss Mason's room?"

"I found Miss Mason dead at eleven-forty-five this morning," I said. "She was lying on her bed in her birthday suit with a knife in her chest."

"Those are big facts, Joe. How about the other considerations? What else did you find?"

"In the room," I said, "I found a box of cookies, a nightgown, some slippers, a dressing gown—"

"And?"

"And some footprints on the window sill."

"Yes. And what else?"

"What else? That not enough?"

"Not quite. Perhaps I should put it this way: What did you *not* find?"

"I don't get you."

"You did *not* find two glasses, one of which had at one time contained poison."

"Oh," I said. "Okay. I did not find two glasses, one of which had contained poison."

"What else can you say about your observations?"

"The footprints," I said, "were a woman's, which means that some dame was in the room at some time. Whether that dame was the one who killed the schoolteacher I guess we don't know yet. Also, it was only one foot, the right one, once going out and once coming in."

"Let's not attribute too much importance to that single footprint," Singer said. "I am sure you must often have hopped in and out of windows in such a way as to leave only a single foot's print on the sill. But the fact that they were a woman's footprints is very interesting."

"So whose were they?"

"They were Miss Mason's footprints."

"Miss Mason's!"

"Is that too simple for you, Joe? I'm sorry I can't introduce a strange lady in black. But I am forced to believe they were her own footprints. Maybe I'm stubborn. Maybe I stick to it because it fits my theory."

I looked at Singer. "So she climbed out on the fire escape, naked as a baby, in her little bare feet, where everybody in town could see her—"

"No, Joe. You are still attaching too much significance to aspects of the case which are not really important. You must try to detach the unusual facts of a person's daily life from those that are normal."

"Suppose you detach them for me," I said. "I guess I'm stupid."

"Not stupid, Joe. Just a little impatient. I will try to tell you what I mean. It was not unusual for Miss Mason to be found naked on her own bed. If it had been in some other place, such as the middle of Oak Street, it would not have been usual. But in her own room it was not too startling. You admit that?"

"I guess so. Of course, most people pull the shades down."

"Ah!" Singer said. "You are beginning to see. It was somewhat unusual to find the shade up. That is a fact which should be separated from the more or less normal aspects of the case. What does it suggest to you?"

"I see what you mean," I said. "The shade went up after she was killed. Then who did it?"

"Exactly. Also, she was stabbed with a knife *after* she was dead."

"All right. If she could be stabbed after she died, somebody could have put the shade up after she died. Go on with the rest of it. What are the other strange features?"

"Very well. It was not unusual, as I have pointed out, to find only one footprint on the window sill. But it would have been unusual to find she had gone out on the fire escape without any clothes on. We rule that out. We assume she had something on when she went out."

"Now look," I said. "First you say it's unusual and then you say it isn't. You say look for the unusual things and separate them from the usual ones. Okay. So it would be unusual for her to go out on the fire escape naked, so she put something on. But it would be pretty unusual for her to go out with something on and no shoes, wouldn't it? Those footprints were of bare feet."

"Yes, Joe. We now come to a somewhat more advanced line of reasoning. I admit it would be unusual for most people to go without shoes or something on the feet. Here we have to fill in some details from what we have observed of Miss Mason's particular character. These are over and above traits normal to people in general."

"Oh," I said. "Now we have got character."

"That's right. You found when you examined Miss Mason's room that she was an extremely fastidious person. Everything was neat and in its proper place. Her clothing was spotless. In short, so far as her personal appearance was concerned she was impeccable."

"So."

"Even though it was obviously her bedtime and she apparently had no thought of visitors and was preparing to go to bed, everything in her room was absolutely neat. She was fastidious to a point of mania. Besides, her shoes were not in evidence anywhere in the room. She had already put them away for the night. The fact that she went out on the fire escape at all at that hour of the night was unusual, since there is no particularly lovely view from the Preston Hotel. So she must have gone out suddenly, unexpectedly, as the result of some sort of emergency, or in response to a summons of one kind or another. Therefore it is reasonable, as I see it, to assume that while she would naturally put on something before venturing outside, she would not necessarily put on shoes. Not if she were in a hurry."

"But there were her slippers," I said. "What about them?"

"The slippers are very important, Joe. There were two pairs. One dainty, feminine pair and one utility pair, as you might say. She wouldn't have worn the dainty ones out on a dirty old fire escape. She would have preferred soiling her feet—which she could wash easily—to soiling the slippers."

"What about the other pair?"

"No. Not those either. Those were bath slippers—all right for shuffling about, but not good for hopping in and out of windows."

"All right," I said. "You have convinced me. Now tell me what happened in that room. I believe it all right, but I can't figure it out."

"Very well. From the known facts and on the basis of more or less logical assumptions, let us try to determine what happened to Miss Mason last night."

"In the order of their appearance," I said, "so I can follow it."

"In the order of their appearance. First, we know she had a visitor, in the person of Tommy Rowe, at about eleven o'clock. We know that when Tommy went up to her room he was carrying a package that contained liquor and ice and perhaps a couple of tumblers."

"She might have had the glasses herself."

Singer nodded. "We won't quarrel over that. In any case, Tommy went up to see her and they had something to drink. So we have accounted for the two glasses. We have established the opportunity for poisoning."

"So Tommy poisoned her?"

"Don't be impatient, Joe. We are faced with the fact that Tommy didn't stay long. We have it from two sources."

"That could be a lot of baloney," I said. "Naturally, Mr. Rowe would try to protect Tommy."

"Yes," Singer admitted, "but we are assuming right now that it's true. Tommy and Miss Mason would have had time for two rather quick drinks. They had one, and then Tommy poured another. He drank his faster than she, doubtless because they quarreled and he was angry."

"You think they quarreled?"

"That is the only reason I can think of right now for his staying so short a time."

"Go on," I said.

"Tommy left with the liquor and ice—"

"Because Miss Mason wouldn't have it sitting around. Her fastidious nature—" I said.

"You are learning," Singer said. "That would have been about eleven-twenty. Miss Mason then undressed, preparatory to taking a bath. She hung her things away and put on her dressing gown. It was eleven-thirty. At this point she was interrupted. She was interrupted from outside, from the fire escape, perhaps by someone tapping on her window shade. She went to see who it was. It turned out to be someone she knew, maybe someone she expected to see. She was asked to come outside. She agreed to go and either took her slippers off—if she had put them on—or left them off, and stepped out onto the fire escape. She left the shade down so that the light from the room would not reveal her on the fire escape. She was gone only about five minutes. Then she came back into her room and went ahead with her toilet.

"She put on her bath slippers and went to the bath, which is just beyond the stairway opposite Room 5, without finishing her drink. She planned to finish it when she came back. It took her about fifteen minutes to bathe."

"At least," I said.

"At eleven-fifty she was back in her room. Before she turned back her bed or made other preparations for retiring she finished her drink. By this time the drink was poisoned. It was now twelve o'clock. She finished her drink, set her glass down beside Tommy's empty one, and took off her dressing gown."

"Sounds like a strip tease," I said.

Singer looked hurt.

"Sorry, go ahead," I said.

"She laid the dressing gown down and took off her slippers. She reached for her nightgown. And it was then that the poison hit her. She groped for the footboard of the bed and supported herself around the end of it. She worked her way around to the edge of the bed and fell on it. She rolled over onto her back, but she was so far gone by then that she could not even get her legs straightened out before she died."

Singer stopped. We were in that stretch of country between Preston and the City which was made up mostly of truck farms. It was dark outside and the driver was making good time. We were rolling along the highway at a sixty-mile clip, swaying from side to side. Singer's story had been pretty convincing. I was seeing it all just as it had probably happened. It was impressive. It scared me a little.

"It's a good idea," I said. "But why? Who did it? Why, after she was dead, did somebody sneak in and stick a knife in her? And who called her outside?"

Singer didn't say anything for a long time. Finally he said: "Those are good questions, Joe. I can't answer them. That is why we are going to the City. That is what we are trying to find out."

"And what about Curly Evans?" I asked. "He wasn't poisoned and he wasn't stabbed. Can we figure on a connection between his murder and Marian Mason's?"

"No, we can't now," Singer said. "But we can assume it. It is not an irresponsible assumption. Curly lived in the back room of the same corridor that led to Miss Mason's room. That would put him close enough for it. Not that I think he did it. Even if he had done it, I doubt very much that he would have used poison. Curly was a more direct character than that. Also, when we asked Bill Fogarty for information we were referred to Curly—which means that he knew something about the situation involving Miss Mason. What that situation was we don't know yet."

"It must have been quite a situation," I said. "It killed her."

"That it did, Joe. Now you and I know that Bill Fogarty and Curly were not constant companions, they were not close friends. It is not likely that Bill Fogarty would have confided personally in Curly. They were not enemies, but they were not intimate, either. So we assume that the quarrel between Bill Fogarty and Miss Mason must have involved something of a more general nature than a mere lovers' squabble. It must have been about something that several people knew something about, Curly being one of those who knew. That is not to say that Curly knew specifically what Bill and Miss Mason quarreled about, or even that they had a quarrel at all. But I believe they quarreled about something that was known to certain people in town, Curly being one of them, and I believe Bill Fogarty's telegram was his way of saying to us 'I don't want to talk about it, but if you should ask Curly Evans you would probably get some interesting answers.'"

I looked at Singer for a while. Then I said: "You've really got it figured out, haven't you? I think you know 'who done it,' as they say. Come across. Who was it?"

"If I told you that now, I would be making an accusation that I couldn't support. I'd rather not make the accusation until I can substantiate it. I have a strong hunch that the Hotel Sheraton will furnish some answers."

"What do you expect to find?" I asked.

Singer shrugged. "I don't know. Let's get off the bus and look around."

CHAPTER 10

The Hotel Sheraton was a third-rate dump on the edge of the business district. The only thing that distinguished it from a million other similar spots was a tavern in the basement which boasted an orchestra and dance floor.

We stood out in front and looked at it.

"What do we do?" I said. "Walk in and ask for Sam Granger and Don Eastman?"

"Not right at first," Singer said. "I think we can be more subtle than that."

"Well, let's go have a few beers and look the joint over."

"It is at times like this, Joe," Singer said, "that I am grateful for your presence. You are much more at home in the world of low and fancy bistros than I am."

"No brains," I said. "Just a little experience and a barroom tan."

"You do have brains, Joe. Don't run yourself down. The only difference between us is the way we apply ourselves. We use our mental machinery for different ends."

Which was a very generous thing for Singer to say.

We went into the tavern. It was eight o'clock and the place was hardly awake yet. There were a few people at tables in dark corners and a few at the bar. The orchestra hadn't arrived yet and the dance floor was empty and dark.

We picked a table near the dance floor. From it we could see every door in the place—there were quite a few doors—and everything that went on at the bar. After about five minutes a waitress shuffled up, yawned, and took our order. We asked for beers and she walked away. After another five minutes she came back with the beers. Singer reached for his money, but I kicked him under the table.

"We'll be here some time," I said. "Just give us a check, and come back in about ten minutes."

"Oh yeah?" she said. "You think you can drink a whole bottle of beer without passing out?"

"How would you like a punch in the paunch?" I said.

She snipped away.

"We might have made a friend of her," Singer said.

"Not her. Dames like that don't make friends."

"You are very smart about women, Joe. Where did you learn it? Surely not in Preston."

"Preston is not a bad place to learn," I said. "You can learn a lot in Preston. Of course, there are some details you pick up only in dumps like this. Dames are pretty much the same. What's different is their environment."

"I see," Singer said. After a minute he went on: "Now take Marian Mason. What kind of girl do you think she was?"

"Well," I said, "a smart girl. Not smart enough to keep on living, but smart up to that point."

"I'm serious, Joe. What did you think of her?"

"I didn't really know her intimately," I said, "until after she was dead. And even then it was only for a little while."

Singer sighed.

"I guess it's no use," he said. "I thought you must have some opinion of her. I seem to remember hearing you admire her."

"Oh, I admired her all right. She was lovely to look at."

"I imagine she was."

"You imagine she was! I'm telling you she was. She was the most beautiful thing to hit Preston in my lifetime."

"Do you think she was—promiscuous? Did she have—as they say— hot pants?"

"That I really don't know," I said. "I never got close enough to find out."

"I was thinking of the fact that at the time of her death she was pregnant."

"That can happen to anybody. It doesn't mean she had hot pants. Of course, it doesn't mean she didn't, either. Let's have another beer. And a sandwich. I know you never eat—but I've got to."

"I'll have something when the job is finished," Singer said.

This time the waitress didn't make any cracks. People were beginning to trickle in. I began to notice that guys would come in and sit down for a few minutes, have a drink, get up, and go out a little door in the back corner and not come back. After about six guys had done this I began to figure they couldn't all be going where you'd think. Sooner or later, some of them would have come back.

"Just what are we looking for here?" I asked Singer.

"We're not sure," Singer said. "But you can keep your eye peeled for somebody we know."

"Who?"

He shrugged. "Who knows?"

"I have already discovered," I said, "that there's more to this joint than meets the eye. Why, for instance, do those guys keep going through the little door in the corner? They never come back."

"Suppose you find out, Joe. Ask questions. Look around."

"I don't have much to go on," I said.

"We have to get started," Singer said. "You solve the mystery of the back door and I'll see whether I can find young Mr. Granger."

"I start first?"

"Yes, please."

I got up and wandered away from the table.

* * * *

It was about thirty minutes later that things began to happen to me so fast I lost count. Sometimes I'm still convinced that I was the one who solved the killing of Marian Mason. When I really think about it, though, I have to admit that none of it would have made much sense if Singer hadn't figured it out. I never would have figured it out myself.

I went to the bar, got on a stool, and ordered a highball. There were two bartenders. One of them mixed drinks. The other one stood around, answered the telephone, and talked to the customers. They seemed to get a lot of telephone calls at that place. About every four or five minutes the phone would ring—it had been toned down to a dull buzz—and this spare bartender would pick it up, say a few words, and hang up. Then pretty soon it would happen all over again. The rest of the time he would stand first at one place and then another along the bar and talk to somebody. Usually, after he had finished, that somebody would get up and walk away, and—if I watched—I always saw him go into that door in the back corner, the door nobody ever seemed to come back out of. It dawned on me at last that maybe there was a crap game back there and I should investigate. But I knew I would have to be okay with this boy at the bar before I could get through that door. I knew it because I had seen a couple of boys try it and not make it.

It happened this way: The front door opened. A guy came in and sat down at the bar and had a drink, quick-like. He set the glass down, paid for the drink, and got up. Instead of going out the front door he headed for that back one. Just sailed right along, as if he owned the place. Then, when he got to the door in the back, all of a sudden there was a big citizen there standing right in front of it and this customer banged right into him. He never even got his hand on the knob. The bouncer simply gave him a little twist and the guy turned around, swaying a little from surprise, and wended his way out into the street.

The first time, that was all I saw. The second time I had a hunch the same thing was going to happen, so I kept my eye on everything, especially at the bar. This time I saw that the guy that came in and ordered a drink didn't say anything to the boy at the bar. He had his drink and then, like the first guy, he got up to go to the back. But when I looked at the mug behind the bar I saw him give a signal toward the back corner of the joint. It wasn't much of a signal, just a slight lift of the right hand and a chopping motion. Then I watched the back door again and the same thing happened. The bruiser in the corner was suddenly standing there in the way, and the boy who wanted to get through couldn't quite make it, and he, too, went back into the street.

Still, I thought, guys would come in and sit at tables and have a drink and get through all right without coming near the bar.

It took me a few minutes, but I finally got it straight. There were guys who could get in without the password, whatever it was, because the guy behind the bar knew them. There were other guys he didn't know, and they had to have the password. They had to stop by the bar. If they didn't bother to stop by the bar and pass the time of day with the mug there, they just couldn't get it. It was a perfect system. And I saw then that while the extra bartender didn't mix any drinks, he kept busy. He was there to keep his eyes open, and that is no mean task in a place where the lights are low and there are people milling around and the only thing you've got to go on is a little wave of the hand.

So it was clear that before I could learn anything about this dump, the way Singer wanted me to, I would have to get through the little door in the back corner.

And the only way I could get through the little door was to find out what you had to say to the spare bartender. I had to learn the password. So I began to beat my brains out for a way to catch on to the magic words. And in order to help my poor head along I bought another drink. I hoped Singer wasn't impatient. This might take me some time.

This little hotel is getting to be an interesting place, I thought, and drank my drink slowly.

A guy came in and sat down on the stool next to me. He ordered a scotch and soda. It came with a swizzle stick. He took the swizzle stick and began tapping on the glass with it, looking around, now and then he'd stop and take a drink, then he'd start tapping again. It made me nervous. I kept wishing he'd stop. I was about to explain to him that I was trying to think and would he mind going somewhere else with that symphony, when something in the way he was tapping stopped me short. There was a pattern in it. He wasn't just tapping for the hell of it, or because he was nervous. He was tapping some kind of message. There would be a couple of short taps, then a pause; and then one tap, and a pause; and then three taps. Then there would be a long pause. And pretty soon he would do it all over again. It went like this: *Tap-tap… Tap… Tap-tap-tap…. Tap-tap… Tap… Tap-tap-tap.*

He would do this a couple of times, then take a drink and look around the room, and then start the tapping all over again. And sure enough, after maybe ten minutes this mug who answered the telephone wandered over, leaned on the bar right in front of the guy sitting next to me.

The customer took another drink, set down his glass, and said, "Room for the night."

The mug behind the bar studied him. Then he asked, "With or without?"

"Without."

"Number 14," said the mug.

"Check," the guy said.

The mug walked away to answer the telephone, and the guy at the bar finished his drink. Then he got up, walked across the dance floor, and disappeared through the little back door. No interference. No trouble.

I ordered another highball, this time scotch, and it came with a swizzle stick. It was probably my imagination, but I could have sworn at the time that the moment the bartender set the drink down for me, that other mug back there began to take more interest. So scotch highballs were maybe a part of the formula, too. I don't know what I'd have done if they hadn't given me a swizzle stick. I could have sat there all night, wondering what was going on.

So after fifteen minutes or so had passed and a couple of guys had come and had a drink beside me and left, I picked up my swizzle stick and started playing chopsticks on the side of my glass. I tapped it out three times and then waited. I waited a long time. The mug wasn't doing anything else, but he wasn't in my direction, either. So I tried it again. The telephone rang and I had to wait for that, and when he got through telephoning I tapped once more. This time it worked.

The face on the guy was something to carry around at Hallowe'en. He put his elbows on the bar in front of me and leaned there and stared at me, and it was all I could do to make myself look back at him. Big nose, blobbed all over his face, pockmarks and thick, blue lips. He was a ghoul. He had practically no neck, and his hands were thick and broad and short, with big freckles on them and bristly hair like a pig's hair.

The sight of him almost shocked me out of my memory, but I managed to hang on long enough to get the first words out.

"Room for the night," I said.

He just looked at me. I was ready to crawl away somewhere and die.

"You been sittin' here a long time. Take you so long to make up your mind?" His voice was like a wood rasp.

Don't try to argue with him, I said to myself.

"Never mind," I said finally. "Room for the night."

After a little while he said, "Gimme a reference."

By this time I was in the water and getting used to it, and also I was a little sore.

"Guy from Freddie's."

"Name?"

"Who knows names at Freddie's?"

Freddie's was a place down on the lake front that I had heard about from Curly Evans. It was one of his hang-outs. Bums, guys off the boats, and general deadbeats hung around there, and Curly had told some tall yarns about the place.

The mug thought this over a little and then he asked,. "With or without?"

I had to think about it. The other guy had said "without." I didn't know whether that was part of it, or whether it had to do with what he hoped to get back of that door. I was curious, but I decided to play it the same way.

"Without," I said.

The mug looked at me for a long time. I had to force myself to look back at him. At last he said, "Number 8."

"Check," I said. I guess I yelled it, because he had started away, and when I said it he stopped and jerked his head around. Those little pig eyes bored into me. That's all, I thought, and braced myself. But then the telephone rang and he went on his way. I finished my drink and got off the stool. As I cut my path to the back door in the corner I glanced over toward the table where I'd left Singer. He was gone.

When I got to the door I saw the big bruiser who had got in the way of the guys who couldn't play. He was sitting at a table with a dame, and his eyes were steady and fixed. I imagined they were fixed on the mug behind the bar.

These guys are like zombies, I thought.

He didn't make a move when I put my hand on the knob of the door and twisted it. It opened away from me and I stepped through.

I was in a narrow corridor with doors along the far side, both to the right and the left. The corridor ran perhaps twenty feet to the left and ended in a blank wall. To the right it ran maybe fifteen feet and made a right-angled left turn toward what would be the back of the building.

One of the doors across from me was open and I looked in. It was a club room of some kind. It was thick with smoke and the lights glared. There was music coming from a small juke-box in the middle of the back wall. There were tables with drinks on them and people sitting around. A guy was doing a crazy kind of dance in the center of the room. A group at one of the tables, men and women, were laughing at him. He juggled up and down and waved his arms around—not really dancing, just jumping. Another crowd at one of the other tables were swaying back and forth with their arms around each other's shoulders, singing. I couldn't make out the song. It sounded pretty weird. At some places there were couples necking. And I mean necking. Not the gentle kind of stuff you do with your girl in a parked car.

The room was crowded and noisy and smelled bitter. A girl got up from a table, pulled her skirt up above her knees, and began to dance, a funny, shuffling dance. Then a guy who had been sitting next to her got up and slugged her. She fell down and got to her knees. She got up and looked at him, pulled back her leg and let him have it on the shin with everything she had. He grabbed his shin and hit her again. This time she didn't fall down. She staggered over toward the door where I was standing. She was laughing. She came out into the corridor, walked past me without seeing me, and went into a room near the end of the hall.

I was about to turn away from this room and go on down the hall when I saw what looked like a familiar face. It was so hazy in there and there was so much moving around that I couldn't be sure.

I stepped inside. There was a table near the door with three girls and a guy sitting at it. One of the girls reached up and pulled at my sleeve.

"Sit down, honey," she said, "and have a drink."

I gave her a look and pulled away, going farther into the room. I was getting closer to that familiar face, and after a couple of minutes I knew I was right.

It was Don Eastman. He was sitting at a table with a little guy in a white dinner jacket and a dame. He hadn't seen me yet.

But I had seen him. The next job was to get him out of there. That might not be so easy.

I pushed past a couple of dancers and stepped up to Don Eastman's table.

"Hello, Donald," I said.

CHAPTER 11

Eastman glanced up. There was a puzzled look on his face at first. Then he grinned and said: "Hello, Joe. Sit down. How'd you get in here?"

I shrugged. "I get around," I said, and pulled up a chair.

"Willie," Eastman said to the punk in the dinner jacket, "this is Joe Spinder, guy from my home town. Joe, meet Willie. Mabel, meet Joe."

Willie, who had a pale smooth little face and big eyes, looked at me and jerked his head. The girl said, "Hi, Joe."

She looked sullen and tired.

"Have a drink, Joe," Eastman said. "Scotch?"

"Sure," I said.

Eastman started snapping his fingers for a waiter.

I looked him over, trying to figure him out. I would never have figured him for a hophead. He was not much of a guy for my money. I had never liked him. He was the fishy-eyed type with a drooling look around the corners of his mouth, and he wasn't popular around Preston. But I had never thought of him as a dope fiend. I had never heard anyone say that about him—and believe me, brother, if anybody had thought that about him, or about anyone else in Preston, it would sooner or later have been mentioned. But here he was in a room full of dopes in the Sheraton Hotel. There hadn't been any doubt about the other people I saw in that room. It put Don Eastman in a very funny position. But I couldn't tell now whether he was hopped or not. I itched to go get Singer and tell him about it so we could get a brain working on it, but now that I had found Eastman, I couldn't afford to leave without him.

The girl named Mabel was staring at me.

"You're not bad," she said suddenly. "Come to the city often?"

"Once in a while," I said.

"Your friend Eastman is quite a boy," she said. "What ever happened to that gorgeous thing he used to bring up here? What was her name—Mason—?"

The waiter brought me a scotch and soda.

"She's dead," I said, picking up my drink.

Mabel blinked. "Just like that?" she said. "She's dead?"

"Just like that. Deader than hell."

Mabel thought it over. Finally she shook her head and shrugged.

"Well—she was too good-looking to live."

I didn't say anything. I noticed little Willie talking very fast to Don Eastman. I couldn't hear what he said.

"Does Eastman know she's dead?" Mabel asked.

"I think he does," I said.

Mabel looked at Eastman. Then she looked at me.

"I don't think it bothers him very much," she said.

Eastman leaned across the table. "You must have got a number when you came through the door," he said. "What was it?"

I remembered the conversation with the mug behind the bar.

"Number 8," I said.

Mabel, staring at Eastman, said loudly, "I hear your beautiful girlfriend is dead."

Don's eyes opened wide and his jaw sagged. But just for a moment.

"You're not supposed to be here," he said to me. "We'd better go down to Number 8. We can talk down there. It's noisy in here."

He got up. I got up, too, thinking, "It's all right with me." We weren't getting anywhere in here. I hoped Willie and Mabel would stay here. Mabel did. But Willie got right up and came along. We swam through the haze of smoke, pushing people out of the way, and got into the little corridor. Don turned left and I followed. Willie was right behind me. We came to the end, where the corridor turned to the left again. Here there were doors every four or five feet on both sides and they were all numbered, odd on the left, even on the right.

We were in the high numbers at this end. As we passed the door of Number 14 I wondered if the guy I had got the password from was in there. But I didn't bother to go in and look. Three more doors and we came to Number 8. Don Eastman tried the knob, it turned, and we stepped in.

It was a small room. There was a frosted window in the wall and below it a tacky-looking, battered studio couch. Some of the fringe was torn loose and hung down around the edges. There were some dirty, lumpy pillows on it that had no doubt been part of the hotel furnishings since 1890. There was a small table beside the couch with a lamp and an ash tray. The lamp was lighted with an amber bulb, about thirty watts. There was a rag rug on the floor and one straight chair. That was all, except for a strange, bitter odor in the air.

Don Eastman sat down on the couch. I sat on the chair. Willie closed the door and leaned against it. I had brought my drink with me. The glass was cool and solid against the palm of my hand. It felt good.

Eastman was looking at me hard. After a while he lit a cigarette, took a couple of drags, and said, "Now what the hell do you want?"

He didn't sound like the old home-town pal now. He sounded edgy and suspicious. I had only one play now—to try to make him think I was friendly until I could get him to Singer Batts.

"I just dropped in to look around," I said, "and have a few drinks."

I took a couple of swallows to prove it. He didn't seem to be impressed. Little Willie, the paleface, leaned against the door and stared at me.

"Who told you about this place?" Eastman said.

"I'm in the hotel business," I said. "We hear about things."

"Did Curly Evans tell you about it?"

"No," I said. I took another drink. "By the way," I added, "Curly's dead."

This got him. He set his drink down on the little stand and his hands gripped the edge of the couch. He closed his eyes tight, then opened them slowly.

"Curly? Dead?"

"Yeah," I said. "Shot. In the back."

Eastman looked around the room. He looked at me. Finally he looked at Willie.

"I've been right here," he said, "in the hotel, ever since noon. Haven't I, Willie?"

Willie didn't say a word. Eastman kept staring at him, but he wouldn't open his mouth. I saw then that Eastman was scared. Things were looking up. Maybe I could handle him after all. I looked at my watch. It was eight-forty-five. A little over three hours to get Eastman back to Preston and D.A. Weaver and to find Sam Granger.

"Look," I said, "Singer's outside. Why don't you come out and join us?"

Again he stared at Willie. It began to look like Willie was giving all the cues around here—and he was pretty close-mouthed.

"No," Eastman said. "I'm tied up—sort of..."

He wasn't tough anymore. He was like a guy caught between the bull and the barbed-wire fence.

"Well, then," I said, "let's go get another drink."

I stood up and started for the door. Willie didn't move. "No drink?" I said.

No answer.

"All right, then.... I'd like to wash my hands. Where do I go?"

I had to get out of there. It was a stalemate. Maybe Singer would have an idea. I would find him and maybe we could coax Don Eastman out of the Sheraton.

"Well?" I said. "Where do I go?"

"Willie will show you," Eastman said.

"What the hell?" I said. "I'm old enough to go by myself."

"It's for your own good," Eastman said. "You don't know who you might run into around here."

"That's no lie," I said. "Let's go, Willie."

Willie stepped aside to let me go through the door, and I went out into the corridor, hearing him close the door behind me.

"Down the corridor to the left," he said.

When we came to the end of the corridor, I started to turn to the right, which was the direction from which I had come in the beginning. But Willie put his hand on my arm and said, "This way."

I turned back and saw a door in the corner, where the corridor made the right angle turn. It was marked MEN. That was what I had asked for and that was where Willie was taking me. He motioned with his thumb and leaned against the wall.

"I'll wait here," he said.

"You going to let me go in by myself, Papa?" I said.

He just gave me a dirty look.

I was liking this little punk less and less as time went by. I decided to needle him a little just to see what would happen.

"You ought not to stand here alone, Junior," I said. "They tell me it's dangerous. Come along with big brother. I'll take care of you."

I put my hand on his arm. He looked at me with a face full of hate and slapped my arm out of the way. I laughed.

"Why, you nasty thing," I said. "You slapped my wrist!"

I was hoping he'd make a pass at me after that one, but he didn't. He just kept hating me with his eyes and shut his lips tight. I laughed again and stepped on in under the MEN sign.

As I went in I was already making up my mind what I could say to Singer when I found him—if I could shake Willie. But almost at once I realized this way was no escape. There was one little window with frosted glass, like the one in the room I had left, and it was nailed shut. But even if it had been open I couldn't have got through it.

I got out a cigarette and sat down to think it over. I had the funny feeling that I was only beginning this little adventure. But I had no idea what the next play would be. I didn't know whether it would be made by me or by somebody else. The way things had been going, I figured it would probably be somebody else. I hoped it would be little Willie, but I was afraid it would be another guy.

If only I could get through to Singer, I thought, and then knew I was dreaming. I knew Eastman was suspicious, and I knew Willie's job was to watch over me.

I had finished my cigarette and there was nothing left to do now but go out and watch for the next move.

There was one chance that was worth trying, just in case I was being too melodramatic and had figured it all wrong.

I stepped outside and there stood little Willie, waiting.

"Look," I said, "I've got to go now. Say good-bye to Eastman for me."

I started off toward the little door that led back to the legitimate side of the dive. But little Willie got in front of me. He was smiling with his lips but there was murder in his eyes.

"No," he said. "Eastman wants to see you again. He likes you."

"I like you too, Junior," I said. "But I don't care whether I never see you again. One side—I'm coming through."

I took a step and threw one at his head.

I don't know what happened to that punch. I know it never landed on anything. I don't know just what movements I made, but I felt like I had grabbed onto a ferris wheel. I swung up with it in beautiful shape, but somewhere at the top I seemed to lose my hold and instead of swinging on around with the wheel I dropped straight down. And suddenly I didn't have any wind and a big lump was growing on my forehead.

I lay there a little while, getting my breath back, and then I crawled slowly to my feet.

"Try that one again," I said, "and Papa will spank the guts out of you."

But I was just talking to see whether I still could. He knew it.

"Come on," he snapped, pushing me around to face the other way. He wasn't kidding a bit.

"All right," I said, "if little Donald wants to see me that much."

We went back down the corridor between the numbered doors. At Number 8 he reached in front of me for the knob. I almost took another crack at him, but my head was aching and I could feel loose blood in my nose and my memory was too fresh.

The door opened and Willie gave me a shove. He didn't come in with me but slammed the door shut and I could hear his footsteps going away. I looked around for Eastman and turned a little sick.

There were two people in the room now, and one of them was still Don Eastman, on the couch. The other, sitting in the straight chair and smoking a cigar, was the big, pock-marked guy from out front who had let me into the inner sanctum. Don didn't look at me. He sat hunched down on the couch watching the other guy from the corner of his eye.

The mug looked at me all right—the way you look at a toad or a lizard. I could see that it wouldn't be little Willie I would have to deal with. Maybe that was for the best.

I got out a cigarette.

"Well, well," I said. "Anybody like a real cigarette?"

There was no answer. The big guy kept looking at me steady and straight. Don Eastman didn't seem to have heard me. I lit my cigarette and threw the match on the floor.

The mug took a long drag on his cigar and blew the smoke out slowly.

"Mind if I sit down?" I said, and I did, on the floor.

"Get up!" the mug said.

I decided I would get up, because when I was down on the floor that guy looked too high up. But I waited a little while so it wouldn't be so obvious.

"What are you doing here?" he said, in his wood-rasp voice.

I tried to look surprised. "I just came in for a smoke," I said. "Guy down at Freddie's—"

"Stop it," the mug said. "You never been near Freddie's. You don't know nobody from Freddie's."

"You're wrong there, bud," I said. "I do know a guy—that is, I did. Guy's dead now. Killed—bumped off, only today."

Don Eastman's head jerked up. He gave me a long look and then turned his head.

"What are you looking for here?" the mug said.

"I don't know," I said, and that was the honest truth.

The mug got up out of the chair and came over to stand in front of me. He walked with a light, springy step, like a fighter. The rest of him was anything but light and springy.

"I said what are you looking for here?"

"I said I don't know." It was the toughest thing I had ever tried to do— looking straight into that ugly face.

"Who's with you?" he said.

"Nobody. I'm on my own."

I never saw it coming. It was his left. The back of his hand smashed against my face and I stumbled back and banged my head on the door. He had had a ring on that hand. I felt a little trickle of blood working down toward my lip. I couldn't see anything for quite a while. When I could, he was standing right over me. His eyes were like extra small black-eyed peas.

"Who's with you?" he said again.

Beyond his shoulder I could see Don Eastman sitting there not moving a muscle, and it made me sore. Instead of answering his question, I kicked the mug in the stomach. I kicked as hard as I could and I heard him grunt. He backed away. There was enough room now for me to slide out and get to the chair. But there wasn't much time. That kick hadn't been enough to hurt him. I'd only taken a couple of steps when he was back again.

At first I tried to box with him. It was like sparring with a mad bull. He outweighed me seventy-five pounds and he was using every bit of it. He hit me in the belly twice and then started in on my face. I ducked out from under once and let him have one on the nose, but it only made him madder. My ears began to ring and the red stuff was flooding out of my nose and I felt like every bone in my head was broken. I couldn't hold my arms up any longer and I started to slip down to the floor. He stopped then and dragged me up to my feet and held me against the wall with one hand on my collar.

"Talk," he snarled. "Who's with you?"

Don Eastman piped up. "I know who's with him," he said. "It won't do you any good to beat this guy up. He's too dumb to give you any trouble."

"Shut up," the mug said. Those were his two favorite words. And to me he said, "Who's with you and what are you looking for?"

"Try something else," I said. "This is getting monotonous."

So he let me have it again. First with the back of his hand, then with the flat of it, back and forth, until I lost count. He had knocked all the fight out of me. All I wanted was to pass out. I kept thinking, "Singer, you better get out of here—I wish I could let you know—you better get out of here," and then finally, as I had wished, I passed out. The last thing I remember was Don Eastman's pale, thin face staring at our little scene with his mouth open and his eyes scared.

CHAPTER 12

I never believed it when I read in the mystery books about how a guy would get knocked out and come to in a strange place just in time to hear the straight dope and figure everything out. But I swear that's what happened to me. Not that I figured it out, but I did get in on some stuff that helped a lot later.

I don't know how long it was. It seemed like I'd been blotto for a couple of years. But when I began to wake up the first thing I heard was that mug's rasping voice and then Don Eastman's, and I thought I was still in Number 8.

I wasn't. I was in a different room. It had a moist, dank smell and I was lying on a stone floor. I opened my eyes to slits—it nearly split my head open—and took a peek.

It was a big room. I was lying against the wall on one side. In the middle of the room stood an old steel desk. Near the desk were a couple of chairs. The mug was sitting at the desk and Don Eastman in one of the chairs. Also present was my little Pal Willie, still dressed in his white coat. And there was another guy, just as big as the mug that had beat me up, only better looking. The only light in the room came from a lamp on the desk, but it threw a pretty big glare. I closed my eyes to relieve the pressure inside my head and listened. I guess the other big boy had just come in. The mug behind the desk asked, "Didn't you find that other one yet?"

"No," the guy said.

The mug swore.

"He couldn't get out. He's in here somewhere. Get everybody on the prowl—the dames too. I want to talk to him."

I said a silent prayer for Singer. I knew what kind of talker this lad was.

The other guy went out through a heavy door in the wall opposite the spot where I was lying. The mug started in on Don Eastman.

"Listen, hophead—" he said.

"I'm not a hophead, and you know it," Eastman said.

"Shut up. You'd be better off if you were. Who was this guy got knocked off in that little hick town of yours? The one this punk was talking about upstairs."

"It was a guy name of Curly Evans."

"He the one came snooping around here a while back?"

"Yes."

"The bald-headed guy?"

"Yeah."

"What was his racket?"

"He didn't have any racket that I know of. He just worked for a living."

"If he didn't have no racket, then why'd he get knocked off?"

"I told you I don't know."

"You kill him?"

"Certainly not," Don said.

"Yeah," said the mug, "the same way you didn't kill that schoolteacher that got croaked last night."

"I didn't do it," Don said. "I don't know anything about it."

"Where'd you get that wad of dough you've been flashing around here?"

"What dough?"

"Don't give me that," said the mug. "I seen it. You must have two thousand smackers in that wallet."

"I made a few sales," Don said. "That's all. They really go for those smokes."

The mug laughed.

"A few sales," he said. "Hear that, Willie? A few sales, he says."

Little Willie laughed too—"Heh-heh-heanh," like that.

"Why, you haven't sold enough hay in that dump to pay expenses," the mug said. "You were going to work that territory like a fine-tooth comb, you said. Hell, those hicks wouldn't buy penny pencils from a blind man. First place, they got no money."

"Look," Don said. "It takes a little while to get started. You have to be careful in a small town. I've made a lot of little sales to the high-school kids."

"Yeah, yeah. Two bits a throw—you call that business?"

"Look—if you'll just give me a chance—"

"A chance—Oh, Christ! I always said you didn't have any business trying to peddle dope in a hick town. Now I'm sure of it. And goddam it, I don't trust you anymore."

He was beginning to sound pretty mean again, and it looked like Don Eastman might be in for a little of that special conversation. After what I had been hearing, I couldn't bring myself to feel very sorry for Eastman.

"And that other dope you brought down here, that banker's kid," the mug said. "He's probably spilled to his old man already. If his old man tips off—"

"He hasn't said a word to his old man," Don said. "He's too scared. The scandal would ruin him. You don't know what it's like in a little town."

"I know what it's like in that town, and I don't like it. You're through here, Eastman, you might as well know it. And you know how things will go if you talk."

"Now wait a minute," Don said. "I've done a lot of business for you. What about that big order for the guy on the farm outside of town? He even mortgaged his place to get the stuff. That was a nice piece of business. And as soon as they get started, the cigarettes will go like hell. And I've got a girl lined up for you too. I'll be able to bring her in any day now."

Oh, Don Eastman, I thought, if they don't kill you first, I will—if they don't kill me first.

"A girl, you say," the mug laughed again. "I seen enough of your girls. That schoolteacher was going to be wonderful. Then you get to her she's going to have a kid—what about that?"

"But I—"

"Aw, shut up. I'm sick of listening to you. You're even dumber than I thought. I'm giving you a chance to get out of this racket free. I'm the only guy in the world would be sucker enough to let you walk out of here alive. And you don't want to quit. My God! Where's that other guy they're looking for? Why did I ever let a bunch of yokels from some goddam hick town—I ought to be hung—"

"You want me to go look too, boss?" said little Willie.

"Shut up," the mug rasped. "Shut up and let me think."

Little by little my strength was coming back. I was getting cramped lying in one position, not daring to move, but I had to wait a little while longer. I was hoping Willie would leave. But he just kept hanging around. I had heard a lot of stuff about Don Eastman but I couldn't put it together yet. It was pretty dirty stuff and I could hardly believe it. But that ugly mug wasn't the type to kid, and I had to believe it.

So Marian Mason was pregnant by Don Eastman. And it was Don who had been leading Tommy Rowe astray, along with Marian. And all of a sudden, Don Eastman had a wad of dough. And somewhere in here Curly Evans was supposed to fit. But where?

I wasn't up to much thinking yet. I tried to relax inside and gather up a little more energy.

"If these guys tip off the Feds," the mug said, "you'll go to the can along with us, you know."

"They won't tip anybody off," Don said. "You can scare them out of that. They're just a couple of hicks."

"Scare them hell," the mug said. "I'm going to see to it that they never get back to that little dump. I should have done that before, when that bald-headed lug came snooping around here. He had plenty of stuff on us. Thank God somebody rubbed him out—saved me the trouble."

"He wouldn't have made any trouble," Don said.

"Hell," the mug said, "he's probably made trouble already."

I wondered what time it was. I opened my eyes again and saw Willie staring at me—full in the face. I blinked and held my breath. After a couple of years he looked away. I had a cramp in my right leg, which was bent under my left one, and the more I thought about wanting to stretch it out the more it hurt. I knew that before long it would force me to move whether I wanted to or not.

"Go bring that kid in here," the mug said.

Willie got up and went out. I waited for the door to slam. That would cover up the noise I would make when I straightened out my leg.

He didn't slam the door. He eased it shut. It didn't make a sound, and the cramp in my leg got ten times worse.

"What are you going to do with him?" Eastman said.

"Shut up," the mug said, in his usual form.

My leg began to get numb, which would have been line, except that it wouldn't do me much good that way. I might have to use it. My head felt better now, but my back ached and there was a hard knot in my chest. The floor was cold and damp.

Maybe, I thought, now is the time to move, before Willie comes back. Maybe I can trick this mug into stubbing his toe.

But it was just about this time that Willie came back, pushing somebody along in front of him.

They crossed the room from the door to the mug's desk, and when they got into the yellow circle of light the lamp threw I saw that the newcomer was Harley Granger's boy, Sam. He hunched up to the desk, his hands in his pockets, and stood there looking at the mug. He had an awful load on.

The mug looked him over for a while and then said, "You know this guy?"

Sam Granger looked at me and nodded.

"Who is he?"

"He's Joe Spinder."

"He from your home town?"

"Yeah." The Granger kid's voice was thick, and it took him a long time to get the words out.

"Is he a cop—a private dick, or something?"

Sam thought it over. He shrugged. "I guess not. Not as I know of."

"Then why'd he come around here?"

Sam shrugged again. "Maybe he came to find me."

"Why should he go looking for you?"

"I don't know. He put me up in his hotel last night. Maybe he feels—res-responsible for me." Sam began to giggle. "Responsible—Sounds silly, don't it?" He giggled some more.

I cussed out the pain in my leg and my headache and the hard floor and thought, *It's about time somebody got responsible for you.*

"Shut up that laughing," the mug said. "You and this guy"—he jerked his head toward Eastman—"are pals, that right?"

"Sure," Sam said. "Good pals."

"Did you know he killed that schoolteacher in your town last night?"

"I did not—" Eastman started to get out of his chair. The mug pushed him back down.

Harley Granger's boy stiffened. You could see fear sobering him up—but fast.

"He—killed her?" he said, staring at Don Eastman.

"Sure," the mug said. "He killed her."

"Did you kill her, Don?" Sam Granger said.

"No," Eastman said. "You know who killed her. You did it. You were doped up."

"No—no—I couldn't—"

"You were out of your head," Eastman said. "You didn't know what you were doing."

Sam Granger started around the corner of the desk toward Don Eastman. Eastman got up out of his chair.

"You can't say I killed her," Sam said. "You killed her yourself."

"I saw you sneaking out of her room," Eastman said. "After you sneaked out of the hotel this morning I went in your room and found bloodstains on the bed."

Sam Granger was getting frantic. You could tell by the way he kept looking around the room—trying to find somebody to help him. I caught him looking at me and I had to fight to keep from blinking. My heart was pounding so hard I was sure they could hear it.

"Where's Roy Blake?" Sam said. "He knows I didn't do it. I'll find him. He knows—"

"He's probably ratted on you already," Eastman said. "Anyway, you can't go back to that town. They'll nab you right away."

"I've *got* to go back," Sam said.

"Why?"

"Because—it's where I live. It's—my father—"

"You wouldn't live long if you went back," Eastman said.

"I didn't kill her," Sam said. "I know I didn't."

"You're crazy," said Eastman. "I practically saw you do it."

"Then why didn't you stop me?"

Don Eastman shrugged. The mug was leaning back in his chair, watching. He seemed to be getting a kick out of it. Little Willie sat on the corner of the desk.

Suddenly, without any warning, Sam took a poke at Eastman. It caught him on the side of his head and he stumbled backward. It made Eastman sore enough to fight. He came back, plowing into Sam. Willie started to slide off the desk.

"Wait," the mug said. "Let's see if the punk's any good."

The punk was either pretty good or pretty desperate because he crowded Eastman all the way. It made me nervous. They kept working over my way. I didn't want them falling on me. I needed what strength I had left.

Sam was slugging Eastman in the belly again and again and pushing back toward me steadily. The mug was laughing. I could hear it over the sounds of their heavy breathing.

I had braced myself against the shock of feeling Don's foot in my face when the mug's voice rasped, "That's enough. Stop it."

They did. And just as they stopped, the door opened and somebody walked in.

It was Singer Batts.

He was all alone, and he stepped in the room as calm as you please and shut the door behind him. He ambled across the room, smiling a friendly kind of smile, as if these guys were long lost pals.

You poor innocent baby, I thought. Why didn't you stay out of this?

Then I wondered how he'd found us.

For a few seconds nobody said anything. I guess the mug was too surprised to talk. Little Willie just stared. Finally the mug found his voice.

"Who the hell are you?"

"Batts is my name," Singer said. "What's yours?"

The mug looked at Don Eastman. Don nodded his head.

"I'm looking for Joe," Singer said. "Thought maybe you'd seen him. I hope nothing has happened to him."

Then he saw me. I don't know whether it was really the first time he saw me or whether he had seen me from the beginning. But it was the first time he had let it be known.

"There he is," Singer said. "You won't mind if we go now? There's a bus—"

I still played dead. I had no idea what Singer's game was, but I wasn't going to do anything to get the mug stirred up again until I was good and ready.

"Your pal, Joe, don't feel so good," the mug said to Singer. "How did you get in here?"

Singer just laughed. He pointed at Sam. "You would be Harley Granger's boy," he said.

He looked at Don Eastman. The mug looked at Eastman, too, and from what I could see of it, it wasn't a pleasant look.

"Honest to God," Eastman said, "I never told this guy a thing. He just snooped around and found it, that's all. He may be from the country, but he's not dumb. I tried to tell you—"

"Shut up," the mug said. He went over Singer with his eyes. "So he ain't dumb, eh? I think we better work him over a little. Maybe that'll make him dumb. Willie!"

Little Willie stepped up to Singer and slapped him across the face viciously.

Singer just stood there. He didn't even take his hands out of his pockets. He laughed a little.

"You're going to waste a lot of time with that sort of thing," Singer said.

Willie slapped him again. I took advantage of their interest in Singer to draw my feet up into a position that would get me up fast when the time came. I had the feeling the time would come before long.

"Wait a minute," the mug said to Willie, and to Singer, "What's that crack mean?"

"Why," said Singer, "you've a lot of incriminating evidence around here. I'd think you would want to get rid of it before the Federal officers come."

The mug stiffened up in his chair. "No Feds coming around here," he said. "Don't make me laugh."

"They told me they'd be here any minute," Singer said. "I gave them a call ten minutes ago. You can check that fact with the girl at the desk. Of course, she doesn't know whom I called. I didn't put it through the hotel switchboard."

The mug was having a hard time. He didn't like to believe this hick snooper, but he didn't want to get caught with his pants down, either.

"Willie," he said, "check that call. If he really did make one, then start clearing the place out, and right now."

Willie beat it.

Singer moved closer to the mug's desk.

"If you don't mind," he said, "Joe and I will go now." The mug snorted. He reached under the desk and came up with a dainty little automatic that pointed straight at Singer. Singer only moved up still closer to the desk. He seemed to be stalling, and I couldn't figure it out at first. Then after a while I caught sight of his feet.

The cord of the desk lamp—the only source of light in the room—hung down over the back of the desk and plugged in somewhere underneath. There was quite a lot of slack in it where it hit the floor. Singer's foot was crawling toward that cord.

"We'll just stay here awhile and see what happens," the mug said. "If the Feds come, I'll have plenty of time to pull this trigger and get out. And if they don't come, I'll have even more time. I'd like to know how you got in here and how you found out what the racket was." Don Eastman spoke up.

"Maybe I ought to go help clear the place out," he said, getting up.

The mug spit at him.

"Sit down," he said. "You're in the same boat with your two pals here."

"No," Don said, "you can't shoot me. I didn't do anything. I worked for you—I made money for you."

"I'm not going to shoot you," the mug said. "I wouldn't do a thing like that. I'm just going to let you be the one to knock off the two hicks here."

"No," Eastman said, "I won't do it."

"That I know," the mug said. "You won't have to do it. I'll do it. Only we'll make it look like you did it, so you'll get the credit. We'll give you a break. We'll beat you up good—it'll look like self-defense."

Don got up.

"You won't do that to me," he said. "I'll spill my guts. I'll inform on all of you."

"Sit down and shut up," the mug said. Don sat down.

I kept my eyes on Singer's foot. I thought I saw him look at me and I tried to nod at him without making any racket. But the light was dim.

The mug turned back to Singer.

"You're a smart guy for a small-town hick," he said. "Too bad I didn't get to know you sooner. We might have had a great time."

A bell rang softly and the mug picked up the telephone that sat on one corner of the desk.

"Yeah?" he said. "...No Feds in sight? You send Jerry back here quick."

And at that moment Singer's foot tangled with the lamp cord. The light went out, there was the sound of smashing glass, and a shot—then another shot.

I had pulled my legs up when Singer's foot moved and I was on my feet by the time the first shot sounded. I made for the desk and in the dark I banged right into the middle of the mug's back. He turned and I hit him back of the knees with my shoulders. I could hear sounds of scrimmaging across the room and I figured Singer must be tangling with Eastman.

The mug went down on his face and grunted as the wind sagged out of him. I socked him behind the ear and almost broke my hand. He squirmed over onto his back and tried to get up and I hit him again. I could see a little now. The mug reached for the gun that had fallen out of his hand when I knocked him down. I made a dive for the gun and we rolled over. I got up first and kicked him in the jaw. Then I kicked him again. He was a tough citizen. He rolled over and shook his head and started to get up again.

Singer's voice sounded plaintively.

"I'm afraid I've knocked Don out. We'd better be on our way, Joe."

"Just a minute," I said.

The mug was still groggy. I got hold of his ears and banged his head on the stone floor a few times. Finally it didn't move anymore.

"Don't kill him, Joe," Singer said. "We don't have time. We've got to get out and call the Federal agents."

My mouth fell open.

"You sweetheart," I said.

I groped my way toward the sound of his voice. I stumbled over Don Eastman and grabbed Singer's arm for support.

"Where's Granger?" I said.

"I'm right here," Sam Granger said. His voice sounded pretty small. It came from beside me.

"You're coming back with us," I said.

"Look, Singer," Sam said, "do you think I killed Miss Mason?"

I guess even Singer is surprised sometimes.

"Do I think what?" he said.

"Eastman said I killed her," said Sam.

Far away I heard voices.

"For God's sake," I said, "let's go."

"Do you think I did it?"

"No," Singer said. "I know you didn't."

"Can we go now?" I said.

"You take Eastman's head," Singer said. "I'll take the feet."

"You know how to get out of here?"

"Yes. It's only a few steps to the alley. We're on the ground floor."

I grabbed Don's shoulders and Singer took his legs. We pushed through the door into a narrow corridor, lighted by a dull red bulb. Far away we could hear voices. They came closer in a hurry.

"The door at the end," Singer said.

At the end of the corridor there was a door with iron bars running the entire height of it. We carried Don to the door and Singer got it open. Just as we went through I looked back. Far down the corridor I could see the shapes of two guys coming toward the door of the room we had just left. One of them was wearing a white coat.

"That little Willie," I said. "I wish he'd come back a little sooner."

"What was that?" Singer said.

"Nothing," I said. "Just saw a familiar face."

CHAPTER 13

The alley was littered with rubbish and there were deep ruts. We stumbled around a lot, but managed to get Eastman out to the street. We stood him up then and I put one of his arms around my shoulders and supported him while Singer stepped out on the pavement to hail a cab. Sam Granger stood around, not saying anything. Once in a while he would start to help me with Eastman, but he wasn't much good to me. He was completely sober now, but shaky. Singer finally got a cab to stop and we pushed Don into it.

"Passed out," I said to the driver. "Had to take him out the back way."

The driver nodded and started off. We headed for the Greyhound Bus Depot. Sam Granger sat on the edge of the seat near the door.

We didn't talk in the cab. Most of the time we spent trying to keep Eastman upright. He was really out.

At the bus depot I saw by a clock in the waiting room that it was ten-fifty. I felt more like five o'clock in the morning.

If we took the eleven-o'clock bus, we'd get to Preston about two minutes before twelve.

We sat down and propped Eastman up between us.

"What did you hit him with?" I said. "The desk?"

"I kicked him," Singer said, looking ashamed.

I had to laugh.

"You look terrible, Joe," Singer said.

"Yeah?" I said. "You don't look like Tyrone Power yourself."

"I've got to find a telephone and call the narcotics agents," he said. "You stay here with Don and Granger. The only thing you have to remember is that we absolutely have to get him back to Preston by midnight. Don't let anybody interfere."

"All right," I said.

He went away and I sat there, holding Don Eastman up with one hand, cleaning myself up with the other, and watching Sam Granger out of the corner of my eye. People walking by would stare a little and some of them looked disgusted and some of them thought it was funny. But nobody bothered us and we were getting along fine until one of the passersby turned out to be a cop.

He strolled by, glanced at us, and went on a few steps. Then he stopped, looked back, and came over. He peered at me, then at Don, then at Sam Granger. He asked, "What's the matter, son? Been in a fight?"

"Fell down," I said. "Friend here passed out. Fell down trying to get him across the street. Damn near got run over. You ought to do something about those cab drivers. Much as your life is worth—"

"Passed out, eh?" he said, looking at Don.

He bent down and pushed Don's head to one side and watched it flop back.

"He sure did," I said. "Tried to show off. Boilermakers."

"You going somewhere? Can't just sit here, you know. This is a bus station."

"We live in Preston," I said. "We're taking a bus at eleven o'clock, little local bus, runs to Montpelier."

"Got any tickets?" the cop said.

I was scared for a minute. Then I remembered I'd bought a round-trip ticket from the driver when I got on at Bridgeville. I dug around, found the return stub, and handed it to the cop. I started going through Eastman's pockets.

"He's got his own," I said.

"What about you?" the cop said to Sam Granger.

Sam started fumbling through his pockets. "Sure," he said, "some-where…"

He didn't find anything, and I wasn't finding anything on Eastman either, but after a minute the cop said:

"All right, son. Hope you get home safe. You young fellows do too much drinking. Ought to be careful, get in trouble."

"Yes, sir," I said, and he walked away.

It was three minutes to eleven when Singer came rushing up.

"Did you get some more tickets?" I said. "There are four of us now, you know."

"I forgot," he said.

"Yeah," I said. "You go get two more tickets. I'll take little Donald and Sam here out to the bus."

Singer dashed off again. I hauled Eastman out to the platform and found the Montpelier bus. Sam stayed right behind me. The bus, luckily, was empty. Few people rode that bus anyway, and hardly ever at that time of night.

The bus driver looked at me kind of funny, but I grinned at him and handed over my ticket. The driver looked at Eastman.

"Passed out," I said. "Trying to get him home."

The driver didn't laugh. "You country boys ought to stay away from the big city," he said.

"All right," I said. "Anything you say. I don't want any trouble. I had enough."

"You look like it," the driver said. "What about fares for these guys?"

"There's another fellow coming," I said. "He'll have two tickets extra."

"He'd better get here," the driver said. "Time to go."

"Any minute," I said. "Any minute."

I staggered to the back seat with Eastman and dumped him. He was beginning to come around now. Every once in a while he'd move his head and groan. Sam Granger sat and stared at him. Sam's face was white as milk.

Singer came scrambling onto the bus just as the driver shifted into low. He hurried back to our seat and flopped.

"I see you made it," I said.

He looked hurt.

"Don't berate me, Joseph," he said. "I'm not used to these late hours."

"Forget it. Did you get hold of the Feds?"

"Yes, I did."

He didn't sound happy about it. When he didn't say anything more I got suspicious.

"Everything all right?" I said.

"Oh yes. Everything is fine."

"Then what are you acting so funny about?"

"Well, it's only a little thing—maybe I'm nervous."

"I'm nervous as hell," I said. "What is it?"

"They didn't like it very well when I told them we couldn't wait, but would have to go back to Preston."

"Oh," I said. "They didn't like that... You didn't by any chance mention that we had one of their key witnesses with us?"

"Well—yes, I did. I mentioned that."

"Great God Almighty," I said. "The F.B.I., the F.B.I.—" It was all I could think of to say.

"Not the F.B.I., Joe. It's the Treasury Department that handles narcotics."

"Oh," I said. "Then it's all right. An entirely different branch of the Federal Government."

"Don't be sarcastic, Joe," Singer said.

"So sorry. The prospect of spending the next ten years in Alcatraz unnerved me."

"You won't go to jail," he said. "The officers will understand when they see we needed Don in order to solve a murder case."

"And suppose," I said, "the murder is not solved?"

"Have no fear, Joe."

"You know who did it?"

"I'm certain."

"Who?"

"Suppose you tell me what you heard in the hotel," he said. "While you were apparently unconscious."

"All right," I said.

I told him what Don Eastman and the mug had talked about. I told him about the girl Don said he had ready to turn over to the boys. Singer made a sad face. I told him about Curly snooping around the place. I told him about the wad of dough Don had suddenly flashed.

"Was anything said about whether the money was crisp and new or whether it was just ordinary old bills?"

"No," I said.

"We'd better find out," Singer said and started looking for Don's wallet.

"Hell," I said. "Money's money."

"Of course," Singer said.

He found the wallet and opened it. It was loaded with dough. They were mostly big bills, fifty—a hundred—. It was all bright and new and crisp.

"Look at that spinach," I said.

"You don't make money like that working in a bakery," Singer said.

"No, you don't," I said. "And he didn't make it working for the drug racket either. That mug in the hotel was just as surprised about it as you are."

Singer put the money back into Don's wallet. Then he called out to the driver, "Will you stop for ten or fifteen minutes in Bridgeville?"

"That depends," said the driver.

"Would you?"

The driver took out his watch.

"I'm ahead of schedule," he said. "I could stop for maybe ten minutes."

"I wish you would," Singer said. "I've a telephone call to make before I get to Preston."

"I'll think about it," the driver said.

Don Eastman opened his eyes and looked around. He didn't seem to like what he saw.

"Go back to sleep," I said. "You got nothing more to worry about."

He didn't answer.

I had a stiff neck and my head was still throbbing. The cuts on my face where that big mug's ring had hit me smarted, and my eyes were puffy and heavy-lidded. I was a minor mess.

I lay back in the seat and closed my eyes.

The last thing I heard was Singer talking to Sam Granger. Sam didn't tell him anything I hadn't heard or figured out. Then I fell asleep.

The next thing I knew Singer was shaking me, saying: "Come on, Joe, we're in Bridgeville. Have to make a phone call. Help me with Don."

I was sleepy. "Can't we just sit here and wait for you?" I said.

Singer shook his head. "I want Don to hear this conversation."

I struggled to my feet and shook Eastman until he opened his eyes.

"Get up," I said. "We're taking a little walk."

Don groaned and grabbed the seat with both hands.

"I won't go," he said.

I didn't have much patience left. I'm not long on patience anyway—as you may have noticed.

"You'll go," I said, and I jerked him up by the collar. "Move now, or I'll beat you to a mess of pulp."

He tried to hang back some more, and I cuffed his face.

"What are you training for, Joe?" asked Singer. "The Gestapo?"

"You want him to get off?" I said. "Okay. Let me handle it my way."

Singer looked away.

"Come on, Eastman," I said, "let's walk."

He came along then, and we lurched down the aisle of the bus and into the fresh air. It seemed to revive him a little. He shook his head and took a couple of deep breaths. Then he came right along, meek as a baby.

"If you've got any idea of making a break," I said, "forget it. I'm right here all the time."

"Where did you get all that money, Don?" asked Singer.

But Don only shut his lips tight and said nothing.

"Want me to make him talk?" I said.

"No, Joe. A confession should be drawn, not wrung."

"Who said I had anything to confess?" Don said suddenly.

"Nobody," said Singer. "I just thought you'd like to help."

Don's voice was bitter. "What's in it for me?" he said.

"About twenty years in Atlanta," I said.

"Oh, yeah?" he said. But he wasn't that brave really. He was just bragging. He knew it, too.

We went into McCarthy's drugstore. I noticed my car was gone and hoped Elsie Schaffner had got home without cracking it up. When we went in, the bus driver was sitting at the soda fountain having a cup of coffee and a sinker. He looked at us but didn't speak. He gave Don the once-over and then went back to his coffee.

There was a public telephone in the back. We went over there and I pushed Don into a chair right beside it. Sam Granger sat down in another chair and I stood. Singer got out some change and rang the operator. He asked to speak to Doctor Blane in Preston. Then he waited. After a while there were some clicks in the telephone and Singer put the money in. You could hear it clanging. Made a terrible racket.

I heard Singer say: "Hello, Doctor. I'm sorry to bother you at this hour, but I have some interesting things on the murders and I need your help... Thank you. In the first place, is the District Attorney still there?... He is? That's fine. Now then, I wish you would tell him in the presence of some people who will be likely to gossip about it that I know who the murderer is... What's that?... I'm certain, Doctor. Now I want you to do this. I want you to round up certain people who must be in the hotel for me to talk to. Here are their names: Tommy Rowe.... I know his mother is not well, but perhaps one of the neighbors would go in and stay with her.... I want Elsie Schaffner to be there, and Mrs. Coolidge, who runs the bakery. Also Mrs. Fogarty. Those are the ones... What's that? Don Eastman? Don is right here with us. He'll be coming back with us... I don't like to tell you my suspicions at this time, Doctor. I'm going to have to produce some evidence. But I must have these people together in the lobby of the hotel... Thank you. I guess that's all. I hate to ask it of you at such a time, but it's very important. I'll be there in twenty minutes. Thank you very much."

Singer hung up.

"You sounded pretty sure of yourself," I said.

Singer laughed. He looked at Eastman. Don looked bad. He was the color of dirty ashes. I thought his teeth were chattering, but I could have been wrong about that. He sat and stared at Singer without blinking, and his mouth was open.

"Well, Don," Singer said, "let's go home."

I've never heard those words sound so cheerless. Don got up out of the chair like a guy in a dream. I took one arm and Singer took the other. Don wobbled when he walked. We had to keep setting him on an even keel. Sam Granger, as usual, plodded along behind us.

The bus driver had got into his seat and was waiting. Singer went in first and headed for the back seat. Don followed him. The driver stopped me as I climbed in and asked in a low voice, "Your friend a dick or something?"

"In a way," I said.

"Was there a murder?"

"There were two murders," I said, with dignity.

"Yeah? Where?"

"In Preston."

"That little hick town?"

"That little hick town."

The driver shook his head and shifted gears. "I'm damned," he said.

"Me, too, brother," I said, and went back to join Singer, Eastman, and Sam.

I guessed that the reason Singer had wanted Eastman to hear the telephone conversation was to get him to talk before we got home. But he never did. He just sat like a dummy, his mouth half open, his face gray, all the way into Preston.

CHAPTER 14

At twelve o'clock exactly we went in the back door, through the kitchen into my bedroom. We could hear voices in the sitting room of the suite. So Weaver and his henchmen were still around.

"Sam," Singer said, "you keep your eye on Don Eastman and stay right here till I call you. Joe and I have to make a little conversation with the county attorney."

I followed Singer into the bathroom. He put his hand on my shoulder.

"This won't be easy, Joe," he said. "The murderer of Marian Mason didn't leave any positive clues. The evidence is circumstantial. He's going to have to be trapped, and I think I can do it. I need your help."

"I'm still breathing," I said.

"Good. The switch-box for the hotel is in the wall just under the stairway, as I remember."

"That's right."

"It opens from the back wall of the lobby?"

"Yeah."

"This is what you're to do…"

He told me. Then he said, "And now we confront Mr. Weaver."

He opened the door and we stepped into the suite. Weaver and the uniformed cop were there. Mr. Pfeffer, the salesman, was still present, minus the handcuffs. When the bluecoat saw me he made a noise and started up out of his chair. Weaver motioned him back down.

"Hello, wonder boy," Weaver said. "I hear you've got it all figured out."

"Thank you for waiting, Mr. Weaver," Singer said.

"Well, spill it," Weaver said. "I've got to get along. Doctor Blane told me you'd asked him to set your little scene. I don't like it, but I've gone this far… Let's get going."

"First there are some questions I want to ask you," Singer said.

Weaver's eyes widened. "Ask me!" he said. "I didn't kill anybody."

"Of course not," Singer said—and waited.

Weaver sighed and settled back in his chair. "All right," he said.

"I suppose," Singer said, "you've begun an investigation of the murder of Curly Evans?"

"Sure," Weaver said.

"Our salesman killed him, too?"

"Of course not," said Weaver. "That's an entirely different case."

"Maybe," said Singer. "Anyway, I'd like to see the list of things you found on Curly after his death."

"Now you're not going to mess around with that case," Weaver said.

"I think it's the same case," Singer said.

"What makes you think it's the same case? He was shot. The Mason woman was poisoned."

"Yes," Singer said. "You found the gun that killed Curly?"

"Not yet," Weaver said.

"Did you find anything?"

Weaver flushed. He pointed to a manila envelope lying on my desk. "It's all in there," he said.

Singer opened the envelope and took the things out. There was the usual stuff: a key ring, a knife, some nails and screws, a wallet. Singer opened the wallet. There were a driver's license, a draft registration card, some odd bits of paper with scribbling on them, a few bills, and a piece of paper that looked like a check. Singer opened it up and spread it on the dresser. It was a draft on the First National Bank for one hundred dollars.

"Hm," I said. "Looks like they paid him in advance for the work at the tourist camp."

"Yes," Singer said.

He put all the stuff back in the envelope and turned to Weaver.

"I've brought with me Donald Eastman, who works in the bakery. Do you want to question him?"

"Certainly," Weaver said.

"Please get Eastman," Singer told me.

I went back into my bedroom and nodded at Sam Granger.

"Bring Eastman into the sitting room," I said.

Sam was certainly being a good boy. He got right up, took Eastman's arm, and led him in.

He didn't have any fight left. He stood in front of Weaver s chair, his hands in his pockets, his shoulders slumped, staring into space.

But Weaver was looking at Sam Granger. "Who are you?"

"Sam Granger," the kid said.

"Are you one of the boys that stayed in the hotel last night?"

Sam nodded. Weaver looked at his cop.

"Go get that other kid," he said.

The uniform went out. Weaver turned to Eastman. "Your name Eastman?"

Don nodded.

"You work in the bakery?"

He nodded again.

"You ever see this salesman before?"

Don turned his head slowly and looked. Then he shook his head.

"You sneaked out of here this morning and went to the City?"

Don nodded.

"What for?"

No answer.

"What for?" Weaver repeated.

Don didn't even open his mouth.

"Ask him if he has plenty of money," Singer said.

"Have you got plenty of money?" Weaver asked—then threw Singer a dirty look.

Don nodded again. He looked like he'd been hypnotized.

"Where'd you get it?"

No answer.

"Somebody give it to you?"

Don shook his head, then nodded. Weaver had got to the end of the road. He couldn't think of another thing. He turned to Singer. "All right, smart boy," I said, "You ask the questions."

Singer smiled. "Glad to," he said. "A little later, in the lobby."

"Why the lobby? Why not here?"

"There are some other people I need to question too. There's a pattern to this. It's like a jig-saw puzzle." Weaver sighed.

The door opened and the uniform came in with Roy Blake. Roy had got cleaned up. He didn't look so scared anymore. When he saw Eastman and Sam Granger he started to smile, then changed his mind. Weaver beckoned to him.

"Now that your friend is here," Weaver said, "maybe you'll tell me something."

"We'll tell you everything we know," Sam said.

"Did you know last night that Marian Mason was dead?"

"Yes," Sam said. "We sneaked out on the fire escape and looked into her room."

"You didn't go into her room?"

"No."

Singer broke in. "When you looked into her room, was the shade up or down?"

"It was down," Roy Blake said.

"You put it up?" Singer said.

"Yes," Sam Granger said. "There's no screens on those windows."

"And was the light in her room on or off?"

"It was off," Sam Granger said.

I looked at Singer. Marian Mason could never have turned that light off.

"Go on," Singer said to Weaver.

"Thanks," said Weaver sarcastically. "When Spinder put you up for the night," he said to the kids, "he took your clothes away from you. How did you get them?"

Roy Blake looked at Eastman.

"He helped us," Roy said. "He got our clothes."

"Why?" Weaver said.

"When we saw Miss Mason was murdered," Sam Granger said, "we thought we ought to tell somebody."

"Why did you pick Eastman?" Weaver said.

"We knew he lived in the hotel, right next to the room we were in. Besides—he was a friend of ours. And we didn't have any clothes. We couldn't go wandering around the hotel."

"So you went to his room and told him what you had seen?"

"Yes," Sam said.

"What did he say?"

"He said we'd better get out of town," Roy Blake said. "He said they'd suspect us."

"But we didn't have any clothes," Sam said. "He told us he'd get our clothes for us. Every morning around three-fifteen old Jack Pritchard goes out to the kitchen to get something to eat. It was about three o'clock when we told Eastman about Miss Mason."

"And he went down and got your clothes and brought them up?"

"Yes," said Roy Blake.

"And you went to the City?"

"I did," Sam said. "Roy wouldn't go. I walked to Bridgeville and took the bus from there."

Singer broke in again. "Didn't Don Eastman go down to investigate when you told him about Miss Mason?"

"No," Roy Blake answered. "He just took our word for it."

Weaver looked at Singer. "Anything else?"

"No," said Singer. "I think we're ready to go ahead. Sam, will you take Don Eastman out to the lobby? Then you two boys had better go home and go to bed."

Sam Granger took Don's arm and led him out of the room. Roy Blake followed.

Weaver got up, "Can we start now?" he said.

"Certainly," Singer said. "You go find yourself a comfortable chair. Joe and I will be along directly."

Weaver went out, followed by his pals. Mr. Pfeffer had fallen asleep in his chair. Nobody paid any attention to him.

"All right, Joe," Singer said. "Go find Pete Haley, get him started, and take up your station."

I went out to the kitchen. Sure enough, there was Pete Haley, making himself a sandwich.

"Pete," I said, "when you get that sandwich made, go back your car into the alley behind the bank, head it toward the street, and stay in it."

"Sure, Joe," Pete said. "Say—be all right if I take a glass of milk along with this sandwich?"

"Help yourself," I said, "but get your car ready."

"All right, Joe. Right away."

I left the kitchen, walked through the dining room and past the stairs, and sat down in the lobby near the switchbox.

* * * *

Doc Blane had not only brought all the people Singer wanted, he had even got them seated together, in a little row near the desk, with the curious onlookers behind them and out of the way. Mrs. Coolidge, a fat woman with a goiter, dressed in old-fashioned high buttoned shoes, sat at the end of the row on a sofa that had been pulled around to half face the desk. Beside her, huddled down and looking very scared, was Elsie Schaffner. Next on a small love seat were Mrs. Fogarty and Tommy Rowe; and beyond them, in a straight chair, was Don Eastman.

Behind them stood or sat the curious. Nancy Wheeler was there, peering at everything with her black little eyes. Doc Blane sat over in the corner. Near him stood Mr. Rowe, Tommy's father. There was a low buzz of conversation, but it was hushed. Singer hadn't come in yet.

Over on the davenport near the big east window sat a guy I'd never seen before. He wore a dark suit and a black hat. He sat with his back to the room, looking out the window. Nobody spoke to him and he spoke to nobody.

Weaver and his cronies were grouped together in chairs just behind Singer's principal guests. Jack Pritchard, the night clerk, was behind the desk. He sat with his lips tight together, very disapproving, very glum.

The door of our suite opened and Singer walked in. A dead hush fell over the lobby. Singer ambled over to the desk and leaned on it.

"I'm awfully sorry to have dragged you good people out at this hour of the night," he said. "But it's very important. We've had a double tragedy in Preston, and I know we all want to get it cleared up. There's a lot more to it than most of you people have suspected. I just happened to fall into some knowledge of it. But I want to make it perfectly clear that this is the case of

Mr. Weaver, our District Attorney. He laid the groundwork. Without him, I couldn't have done a thing."

In a pig's eye, I thought.

Everybody turned to look at Mr. Weaver, who beamed a little.

Someday, Singer, I thought, you will undoubtedly be the President of the United States.

"Now then," Singer said, "Mrs. Coolidge—I understand you bought a couple of knives yesterday from a traveling salesman."

"Yep," Mrs. Coolidge said. "Bought two. Little one to slice cookies, an' a bigger one for the bread. Good sharp knives they was, too. Cost me somethin', though. I'm gonna have to up my prices some to pay for 'em. 'Sides, got to buy another one now."

"Is that so?" said Singer.

"Yep."

"You lost one?"

"Yep. Day 'fore yestiddy I bought 'em—bought 'em that mornin'. That night when I closed up I seen one of 'em was gone."

"Which one?"

"Big one," she said.

"It just disappeared?" Singer said.

"Yep. First 'twas there, then 'twa'nt."

"Mrs. Coolidge, was Don Eastman at work the day before yesterday?"

"Yep."

"Thank you, Mrs. Coolidge. Mr. Weaver has ascertained that Miss Mason was stabbed with a knife exactly like the one purchased by Mrs. Coolidge for the bakery." He paused. "However," he went on, "we know that Miss Mason did not die from a knife wound. She was poisoned."

Don Eastman jumped to his feet.

"See—see?" he said wildly. "I told you I didn't do it. I didn't kill her—"

"Sit down, Don," Singer said. "Nobody said you killed her. The interesting thing is that you didn't know until this minute that you hadn't killed her."

I looked at Tommy Rowe. He sat staring at the floor, twisting his hands. He didn't look at Don Eastman.

"I want to turn from the actual killing of Miss Mason," Singer said, "to the reason for it, the motive that lay behind it. This is not going to be very pleasant, but it is necessary if we are to get to the bottom of this mystery.

"I would like to add that, tragic though it was, the death of Marian Mason has made it possible to put a stop to a grave menace that has hung over Preston for the last few weeks.

"Elsie," he said—and Elsie Schaffner turned scared blue eyes up at him—"you were a good friend of Miss Mason's, weren't you?"

"Yes," Elsie said, in a small voice. "She was my Latin teacher. I liked her."

"You went out sometimes with her, didn't you?"

Elsie looked down. "Yes, I did."

"And with whom did you usually go?"

Elsie hesitated. Finally she said, "With Tommy Rowe—and Don Eastman."

"You don't drink or smoke, do you, Elsie?"

"No," she said. "Well—once in a while I would smoke a cigarette when I was out with Miss Mason. But I never drank."

"Once in a while you would smoke a cigarette. Did you buy your own, Elsie?"

"No. The boys always had them."

"I see. Did the boys ever offer you a strange kind of cigarette? A kind you'd never seen before?"

It was getting pretty tough on Elsie. She swallowed hard and didn't answer.

Singer went on, very gently: "I know you never did anything wrong. You didn't commit any crime, and you don't have to be afraid."

She looked up at him.

"How many of these strange cigarettes did the boys give you?"

"Three or four," she said.

"Did you smoke them?"

"Not all the way," she said. "Just a little."

"What kind of cigarettes were they?"

There was a long pause. At last she said, in a whisper, "Marijuana."

The guy in the black hat got up slowly and turned around. He leaned against the big window with his arms folded and watched Singer.

Then I caught on.

"Singer," I prayed to myself and whoever might be listening, "you better be right. You kidnapped their witness. And I helped."

"So Don Eastman and Tommy Rowe gave you marijuana. Did Miss Mason smoke them, too?"

"Yes."

"More than you did?"

"Yes. She liked it, I guess."

"Did she ever offer them to you?"

After a long pause, Elsie said, "Yes. She always had them."

"Do you know whether she offered them to others—to your schoolmates?"

Elsie twisted her hands. "Yes. She did."

"And did either of the boys give you any cigarettes to give to your friends?"

"Don Eastman did. Tommy Rowe never gave me any," she said. "It was always Don."

"What did he tell you when he gave you those extra cigarettes?"

"He told me to give them away to boys or girls I could trust, and tell them they could get more from him if they wanted them. He told me it was a crime to smoke them and if anybody found out about it, we'd all go to jail, even Miss Mason. But he said they wouldn't really hurt you. It was just a superstition."

I happened to look at Doc Blane when she said that. His face was white. He was twisting his lips and looking at Don Eastman as though he wanted to strangle him. Don's head was sunk on his chest and his hands hung loosely beside him. Tommy Rowe kept staring at the floor.

"Just one more question, Elsie," Singer said. "Did you ever go to the Sheraton Hotel, in the City?"

"No," Elsie said. "The boys talked about it a lot, and I wanted to go, but Miss Mason always said no."

Doc Blane couldn't hold back any longer.

"Thank God she had that much good in her!" he said.

Everybody looked at him. Doc was confused. He covered his face with his hand and cleared his throat loudly.

Elsie lowered her head and began to cry. Big fat Mrs. Coolidge leaned over and put her arm around Elsie.

"Thank you, Elsie," Singer said. "You're a brave girl. You don't have to stay any longer if you don't want to."

After a minute Elsie got up and walked out of the lobby. A man got up from the back of the lobby and went with her. I guess it was her father.

"The Sheraton Hotel," Singer said, "is—or was—a center for the peddling of narcotics. It's not pretty to think that that sort of thing would come spilling over into a nice little town like Preston. But unfortunately it's true. And much as I hated to find it out, I have to say that Don Eastman was responsible for it."

He told about Eastman's connections with the Sheraton mob. He didn't go into detail about the fight we had, which was just as well.

"Now then," he said, "Curly Evans was one of the very few people in Preston who knew all about the Sheraton Hotel, and about Eastman's connection with it, and about the fact that Miss Mason and Eastman and Tommy Rowe had been there. He knew it because he had made it a point to investigate it.

"We all knew Curly. He was a hard-working, decent man who minded his own business. He was not the sort to sneak around sticking his nose in other people's affairs, spying on them, snooping. Curly Evans didn't investigate the Sheraton Hotel out of idle curiosity. He investigated it because he was paid to do so. He did it for hire. And he never breathed a word about it to anybody besides the person who hired him, except one—that one was Bill Fogarty."

"Who the hell is Bill Fogarty?" Weaver asked.

"Bill Fogarty is very incidental to this case," Singer said, "but he is important, too. He is important because he is the first link in the chain of circumstances that led directly to the murder of Miss Mason.

"We already know that Miss Mason was involved with Don Eastman and the activities that went on at the Sheraton Hotel. But there was something else about her that we haven't mentioned yet. It was found that at the time of her death, Miss Mason was pregnant."

Another sudden buzz of conversation. Singer spoke a little louder.

"That is another unpleasant fact that we have to face. Now, as for Bill Fogarty—we know he quarreled with Miss Mason a few nights before the murder. As you know, Miss Mason lived with Mrs. Fogarty before she moved to the hotel. Before Bill enlisted, he used to run around with Miss Mason. They were quite friendly." Singer turned to Mrs. Fogarty, who stared up at him out of wide, innocent eyes.

"You told Joe and me," he said, "that Bill and Miss Mason quarreled one night while Bill was home on leave."

"Yes," she said. "That's right, Singer."

"What did they quarrel about, Mrs. Fogarty?"

He asked it sharply and a little sternly, as though he hardly hoped for a quick answer but was going to try.

He didn't get a quick answer. Mrs. Fogarty fluttered her hands and looked away.

"Well—it was late," she said. "Miss Mason had been out and came in very late. I'd gone to bed. Bill was sitting up, and they talked. But really, I was half asleep and I didn't hear much of what they said. I—"

"I think you did, Mrs. Fogarty," said Singer. "I know it isn't easy for you, but whatever happened was no reflection on Bill, and certainly not on you. It is important that we know why they quarreled."

Mrs. Fogarty shook her head and played with her skirt.

"I'm afraid," she said, "I really couldn't…"

"Miss Mason asked Bill to marry her, didn't she?"

"Oh no!" Mrs. Fogarty looked frightened. "I'm sure—"

"She told Bill she was going to have a baby. Bill said it wasn't his child and she said she'd make the town think it was. Isn't that what she said?"

Mrs. Fogarty looked bewildered. She wouldn't say yes, but she didn't say no, either.

"Then Bill told her he'd heard about her going to the Sheraton Hotel with Don Eastman and Tommy Rowe. He tried to make her see that she was heading for trouble, and she wouldn't listen. She began yelling at him, telling him she'd let everybody know the child was his and she'd ruin him in the Service. Isn't that right, Mrs. Fogarty?"

Mrs. Fogarty sat quite still. After what seemed a long time she said, "Yes. That's true."

"And the next day," Singer said, "you told her to leave your house."

Mrs. Fogarty nodded. "Yes," she whispered.

Singer went over and laid his hand on her shoulder.

"I understand, Mrs. Fogarty," he said. "It was just that you couldn't bring yourself to say it. This town is proud of you and Bill."

That was Singer. What a sweetheart!

Mrs. Fogarty patted his hand. "Thank you, Singer," she said.

Singer went back to the desk.

"I don't know why Curly told Bill Fogarty about Miss Mason and the Sheraton Hotel; but I know he did, because when I wired Bill and asked him what he and Miss Mason quarreled about, he wired back telling me to ask Curly Evans. I never had a chance to ask Curly. The next time I saw Curly, he was dying."

Weaver jumped up.

"Wait a minute!" he said. "I didn't know about all this—"

Singer raised his hand.

"Just a moment, Mr. Weaver. I won't be much longer."

Weaver sat down.

"The scene with Bill Fogarty was Miss Mason's first attempt at what is known, I believe, as a shakedown. Bill Fogarty would have been a good, substantial husband. When she knew she couldn't scare Bill into marrying her, she went after something else. Money. She didn't want to marry the man who was actually the father of her child. But she knew she would need money. She went to the real father for it, because she thought that although he didn't have it, he could get it.

"But he just laughed at her. She was desperate and she threatened to expose him as the peddler of drugs she knew him to be."

Everybody looked at Don Eastman.

"That scared him," Singer said. "He knew she could expose him, and he knew it would go hard for him if she did. So in order to mollify her, he helped her plan still another shakedown, this time with someone who did have the money, somebody who had been seen with Miss Mason even more than Don had."

Now they were looking at Tommy Rowe.

"He thought he had it all fixed up. He thought she would go to Tommy Rowe and that Tommy would either marry her or give her money. But she didn't go to Tommy Rowe. She went to somebody else. And she got paid off. And Don Eastman began to worry, because Tommy hadn't told him whether she had gone to him or not, and he got so worried that he was desperate. So the night before last, Don Eastman stole a knife from the bakery where he worked and at one o'clock in the morning, or thereabouts, he crept down the hall to Miss Mason's room. He saw her lying on the bed and thought she had fallen asleep, or had taken too much liquor. He plunged the knife into her heart.

"On the dresser in her room lay a bundle of money—nice, new, crisp green bills wrapped in a bit of white paper. Don Eastman picked up the money, turned out the light in Miss Mason's room, and went back to his own room. He thought he had killed her. He thought so until tonight when I said she had been poisoned. He thought he had sealed up forever the evidence she had against him on the narcotics traffic.

"But he was wrong. The evidence against him had already been gathered—*and written down*—by Curly Evans. Enough evidence to send not only Don Eastman but someone else to the penitentiary for ten years at least.

"I know Curly Evans wrote it down. I know he carried it with him. Because Bill Fogarty told me that, too. And I know that the evidence somehow got lost when Curly Evans was shot. Joe Spinder and I found Curly in one of the dressing rooms at the tourist camp, and when we carried him out, a sheaf of papers fell from his pocket. We were too busy then to pick them up."

Singer reached into his hip pocket and pulled out his handkerchief. I reached up into the switch-box.

"I know that those papers must still be lying somewhere down at the tourist camp where Curly was murdered. And I think Mr. Weaver and his men ought to go down there right now and get them."

I pulled the master switch and the lights went out. Suddenly it was dark as pitch in that lobby. Somebody screamed—I think it was Mrs. Fogarty. Somebody said, "Goddam it"—and I know that was me. Then I heard Singer's voice say, calmly, softly, "All right, Joe," and I came to life.

I beat it back through the dining-room and the kitchen and into the alley. Pete Haley's car was parked at the entrance to the alley, facing North Street. I opened the right front door and lammed in.

"Okay, Pete," I said. "Start her up."

No answer. I looked at him.

Pete was asleep. He was snoring.

"Goddam it, Pete, wake up!"

I hit him in the ribs with my elbow. He grunted. I saw a car come tearing around the corner by the bank and head north. I got out and slammed the door and ran around to Pete's side of the car. I socked him in the head and in the stomach. He woke up.

"Move over," I said.

I helped him and he crawled out from under the wheel. I saw another car come ripping around that corner as I stepped on the starter. As I got into low a third car went by, and then I was out in the street, cussing at the top of my voice.

Way up ahead I saw a tail-light moving fast and swerving a little as it hit the railroad halfway to the edge of town. I kept my foot down on the floor. Pete's old crate was pretty shaky, but it was big and powerful and moved right along.

Pete was coming to life. He took off his cap and scratched his head and rubbed his face with both hands.

"Where we goin'?" he said.

"See that tail-light up there?"

"Yeah."

"We're going wherever it goes."

"Oh," said Pete. "Goin' north."

"Yeah," I said.

It was going north all right, at about sixty-five miles an hour.

"Say," Pete said, "there's a thirty-five-mile speed limit now, you know."

"I know."

"Better slow down."

"Go back to sleep, Pete."

"Can't," Pete said. "Git nervous with somebody else drivin'."

"Don't be nervous," I said. "This won't last long."

"Hope not," Pete said.

Suddenly that tail-light up ahead seemed to stand still.

I got ready to set the brakes—then it disappeared, and I saw the headlights shift and turn off to the left. That was the tourist camp road and I felt a little guilty when I plowed Pete's tires into that bunch of rocky ruts. I slowed down a little.

But the car ahead didn't slow down. He got into the winding part of the road before I was over the first hump. I missed a rut and swerved, and a branch swished into the windshield, then came through the window and slapped Pete's face.

"Take back a little, young feller," Pete said. "Ain't that much hurry."

"Oh, yes, there is!"

I was in the woods now, bumping and twisting along, and I couldn't see any car ahead of me. I kept thinking: I didn't see any papers in Curly's pocket.... *What* paper?... There *weren't* any papers!... But that Singer—he sure made them think there were... That Singer!

Then we came out into the clearing by the bathhouse and I had to jam on the brakes to keep from plowing into the car. It was a nice new car. I'd have hated to scratch it.

I jumped out and yelled at Pete to come along. There were three cars lined up in front of Pete's. I passed them and made for the bathhouse. There were loud voices coming from the other side of it and one of them was Don Eastman's. He was doing most of the talking. The other voice, I figured out, belonged to Tommy Rowe.

But there were three cars!

"You did it," Eastman was saying, as I came around the corner of the bathhouse. "You killed her. You went up there and had a drink with her and poisoned her."

"You're crazy," Tommy said. "Why should I kill her?"

I stopped to listen. Pete came pounding up behind me, and I grabbed his coat and stopped him.

"That Singer Batts," Don said, "he was just making that up. Marian did try to shake you down. You were afraid to ask your old man for money. You killed her."

"Yeah?" said Tommy. "Then where did she get that dough?"

"What dough?"

"The dough that was on the dresser, that you stole."

"Why, you dirty—" Don took a poke at Tommy.

Then they were all over each other, clawing and yelling and kicking like a couple of schoolgirls. Pete started forward.

"Wait," I said. "Let them go to it. Save us a lot of trouble."

Headlights flashed behind us and a car ground to a stop. I heard Singer's voice.

"All right," I said to Pete. "Let's break it up."

We waded in. I drew Don Eastman. I was getting used to pushing him around. I even liked it a little by now. Pete grabbed Tommy and held him up, with both his huge arms pinning Tommy's tight to his chest. I pushed Eastman up against the bathhouse and held him there.

Around the corner came Singer, Weaver, and the guy in the black hat.

"There's *your* man," Singer said.

The guy in the black hat stepped up to Eastman, flashed a card, and slapped handcuffs on him. The guy looked at me.

"Thanks, bud," he said. "You're tough. How about coming into the Service?"

"No, thanks," I said. "I handled my last narcotics case one minute ago."

He grinned.

Weaver had gone up to Tommy Rowe. The uniformed cop was with him.

"All right, son," Weaver said. "Stick out your hands."

"No," said Singer. "He didn't kill Marian Mason. There's nothing against him."

"Then who in hell did?" Weaver said. "What kind of rat race is this?"

"There goes your murderer—over there."

Singer pointed. A dark figure was skirting the edge of the trees in a wide circle back toward the parked cars. "Wait!" yelled Weaver, starting to run over that way. The figure stopped, turned, and came walking slowly back to where we stood.

"I'm sorry," Singer said and turned his head.

"That's all right, Singer. You had to." It was Mr. Rowe. His voice sounded very tired. "I'll go quietly," he said to Weaver.

For a moment Weaver was speechless.

"You did it?" he said finally. "You killed her?"

"Certainly," Mr. Rowe said.

"And that other guy—Evans. Him, too?"

"Yes. I was sorry about Curly. I killed Miss Mason because I hated her and wanted to protect my son and the town from her. But I killed Curly because I was afraid. I didn't need to kill Curly. I know that now. But I was afraid." He smiled. "Never kill because you're afraid," he said. "It will trip you up every time."

"But the poison," Weaver said. "Do you always carry strychnine around with you?"

Mr. Rowe shook his head.

"Singer figured that out," he said. "He'll tell you about it. I killed Curly with an old gun I've had for years at the bank. You'll find it in the top right-hand drawer of my desk. I haven't even cleaned it."

Weaver took Mr. Rowe's arm and they started off. Then Mr. Rowe stopped and looked back.

"So long, Tommy," he said. "Take care of your mother."

And they disappeared.

Tommy was leaning against the bathhouse. I thought he was sobbing, but I wasn't sure. After a minute Pete cleared his throat.

"Come on, Tommy," he said. "I'll give you a ride to town."

"I've got my own car," Tommy said.

He moved away and disappeared, too. Pete started to follow him, then stopped.

"Joe," Pete said, "will you bring Mr. Rowe's car back to town?"

"Sure," I said. "'Night, Pete."

"'Night," Pete said. He went around the corner of the bathhouse.

I stood there, muttering to myself.

"What was that, Joe?" Singer asked.

"There's still some whisky left at home," I said. "Let's go finish it up."

"I'll go," Singer said. "But I won't need any more whisky. It's carried me through this case."

"All right," I said. "I'll drink yours."

We went over and got into Mr. Rowe's car.

CHAPTER 15

Back in the suite, I'd taken off my clothes and mixed a drink. Singer was sitting at his little work table.

"I still don't see how you knew," I said. "Break down. Let me in on it."

Singer laughed.

"Number One:" he said. "Mrs. Rowe had heart trouble. Strychnine—good old *nux vomica*—is often prescribed. In a place like Preston, with a staunch citizen like Mr. Rowe, it is quite reasonable to assume that Doctor Blane would let Mr. Rowe buy a quantity of strychnine, tell him how to use it, and leave him to his own devices. I don't think he always carried it with him. I imagine he got the prescription refilled yesterday morning. But that isn't important. I was suspicious of Mr. Rowe almost from the start."

"You were?"

"As I have said, you are a high-fidelity reporter, Joe. In that report you did for me this morning you even included the conversation between Mr. Rowe, Mr. Granger, and yourself—about putting the two boys up for the night."

"I don't get it," I said.

"You don't remember? When you admitted to Mr. Rowe that you had taken the boys in, what was the first thing he asked you?"

I scratched my head.

"He asked you, 'What time?' That question didn't fit with the rest of your conversation. At that point, Mr. Rowe wasn't interested in the two boys themselves—he was interested in whether they had been in the hotel during the murder. His 'what time' question showed that."

"Okay," I said. "What else?"

"Number Two: I knew Curly must have been working for somebody. When we found the hundred-dollar draft on Mr. Rowe's own bank, I was sure who it was. Then there was the money Don had, the bright new bills. The bank would be the only place here where you would find so many new, crisp bills of such denominations. I knew then that somebody had been bought off. I didn't think anybody would bother to buy off Don Eastman."

"But if he bought her off," I said, "why did he kill her?"

"He killed her because he knew he couldn't buy her off really. He knew she would come back again and again. He could see Tommy in trouble with the Government, and her blackmailing him. Mr. Rowe is a strong-minded man. He wouldn't have sat around and let anyone blackmail him. Not for long."

"How did he do it?" I said.

"Curly helped him."

"Curly!"

"Curly didn't know it. Mr. Rowe asked Curly to watch Marian for him and let him know when she was in her room. He stood down in the alley and watched Curly's window. Curly gave him a signal, and Mr. Rowe went up to Curly's room. He gave Curly the money and told him to go out on the fire escape and get Miss Mason outside for a few minutes, then give her the money. He said there was evidence against Tommy in her room and he wanted to get it.

"Curly went out on the fire escape and called Miss Mason. She expected Curly to be the agent for Mr. Rowe, so she went right out. Curly stalled around and finally gave her the money. In the meantime Mr. Rowe went down the hall to Miss Mason's room, dumped poison into the glass that still contained some liquor, and left."

"But how would he know she had a glass with liquor in it?"

"He didn't. He had planned to kill her some other way. Probably by strangling. But he found the liquor and decided to use poison."

"What about Mr. Rowe hiding in the bathroom and seeing Tommy come out of her room?"

"That I doubt, Joe. I think they made that up between them."

"Then you think Tommy knew his father had done it?"

"Perhaps."

"Of course, Tommy might have had the poison," I said.

"Mr. Rowe would never have trusted Tommy with it. Besides, Tommy had no reason to kill Miss Mason."

"Then she really didn't try to shake him down?"

"I think she did. But not very strenuously. She knew Tommy didn't have anything in his own name."

I thought it over.

"All right, it sounds logical," I said. "There's one more thing. How did those glasses get out of Miss Mason's room? Who took 'em?"

"Curly," Singer said. "Curly was trying to help Mr. Rowe. He woke up in the morning and started out. He heard Nancy Wheeler scream, and he went down the hall to Miss Mason's room. He saw her dead and he saw the glasses on the dresser. He knew Tommy had been up there and he was afraid he'd be implicated. He took the glasses out of the room."

"How are you so sure?" I said.

"Remember where we found the glasses? Back of the laundry. When Curly came downstairs in the morning, when you were standing by the desk talking to Pete and Harry, he was carrying a bundle of laundry. Remember?"

"Yeah," I said. "I remember."

"I have a question or two for you, Joe," Singer said.

"For me?"

"Yes. How many times did you date Miss Mason?"

I looked at him. "How did you know?"

"Did you ever actually go out with her?"

"A couple of times," I said.

"Was she friendly?"

"Not very."

"Were you?"

"I was friendly as hell."

"I see."

"What about it?" I asked.

"It explains the marriage license."

"It does?"

"Yes. You see, you were someone she could fall back on. If the best deal she could make turned out to be a respectable marriage, she had you. She knew she had you. All she would have had to do would be to turn friendly."

"You're saying she would have married me?"

"Of course. You must remember, Joe, that she was desperate. A woman as desperate as she must have been would have taken any man she thought of. Any man at all."

"Go to hell," I said.

"Undoubtedly," said Singer, bending over his desk.

I finished my drink.

"Aren't you going to bed?" I said.

"Not right away, Joe. I want to make a few notes. I think I've solved this Elizabethan murder we were talking about. I want to pin it down."

I was too tired to argue. I set down my glass and went over to the bathroom door.

"Good night, Singer," I said.

Singer didn't answer. He was making notes at a fast clip. He was settled for another twenty-four hours.

www.ingramcontent.com/pod-product-compliance
Lightning Source LLC
Chambersburg PA
CBHW011448170626
46816CB00008B/2574